CYNTHIA HICKEY

SECRETS OF MISTY HOLLOW

By Cynthia Hickey

ISBN: 978-1-952661-15-0

To avid readers everywhere!.

Susan Reece's hand trembled as she touched the large envelope the detective slid across the desk. Her mouth dried, making speech impossible. She dropped the envelope into her purse and stood on shaking legs.

"I cannot stress enough the importance of never using your or your daughter's real names again. You wanted a remote location to live. Well, you've got one," the detective said, taut lines framing his mouth. "We can only pray it's enough to keep you safe. Here is a cell phone and the number to call when you arrive at your destination. We've transferred the phone into your new name, and it's paid up for six months. You'll have to find a job." He stood and held out a hand. "Good luck, ma'am."

She gave a quick shake of his hand and rushed from the room. Outside, she leaned against the wall and fought to control the tremble in her breath. What had she been thinking to leave a world that gave Kayla everything she needed and then some? Who leaves a life of luxury?

Still, Susan couldn't live that lifestyle anymore. Anthony would never give up looking for them. He wouldn't be pleased to lose his only child.

A semblance of control gained, she dashed to the parking garage and the Mercedes—a present she'd received after giving birth to Kayla. One more thing she'd have to leave behind. She stopped and listened for any sign she wasn't alone in the garage at ten p.m. Two cars sat there, hers and the detective's. She raced to the Mercedes and slid in, locking the door.

It took several tries for her fingers to grasp the key and start the engine. Time was of the essence. Not only did Susan need to pack what she could carry, but she needed to study the file in her purse. Her new identity. Her new home.

She parked behind the motel which had been home for the last few months and hurried into the tiny room she shared with her five-year-old daughter. "Thank you, Mrs. Johnson."

The old woman sniffed and nodded. "I don't approve of mothers running around at all hours of the night, leaving their children with virtual strangers."

"I didn't have a choice." Susan pulled articles of clothing from the dresser and tossed them, unfolded, into suitcases. A bus would be leaving the nearby stop in thirty minutes.

When she'd packed what little they possessed, she gently woke Kayla. "Come on, sweetheart. Time for the next part of our adventure."

"Are we going home now?"

"To a new home." Susan forced a smile. "We're

going on a bus so we have to hurry." She handed her daughter the stuffed bunny she never went anywhere without. It was too precious to leave behind.

With a suitcase in each hand, Susan guided Kayla out the door and to the bus stop. Her skin prickled. Any second she expected one of Anthony's goons to pull up and order them into a car. The tension in her shoulders didn't ease until the bus stopped and opened its doors.

While Kayla curled up in her seat, using the bunny as a pillow, Susan finally opened the envelope in her purse. Driver's license, birth certificates, everything she need for a woman named Sharon Marshall and her daughter Karlie. They had a three-day journey to the small town of Misty Hollow, high in the Ozark Mountains. A credit card and a few hundred dollars in cash accompanied the important papers.

Susan sighed and stared out the window, tears streaming down her face. She'd done it. Left behind a corrupt lifestyle to start anew. It would work. It had to. She'd given up too much to fail now. The moment her head touched the seat back, her eyes closed.

When the bus stopped in Misty Hollow, Susan was more than ready to get off. The sign had stated the population to be 2300. "Stay close to me, Karlie. Remember, that is your name now. Can you do that for me?"

Karlie nodded, eyes wide. "There are a lot of trees, Mommy."

"Yes, isn't it wonderful?" Susan/Sharon felt like a fish flopping around. Being a city girl, she'd never been in a town this small or surrounded by so much green. The excitement bubbling up inside surprised her at being in a new place, starting a new life. Now to find someone who could take them to their new home. She pulled a slip of paper from her pocket and dialed the number. "This is Sharon Marshall."

"We'll have a local pick you up in less than ten minutes. Delete this number." Click.

They stood in the shade of a large tree until a rusty Ford pulled in front of them. "You the Marshall lady who bought the old Rogers cabin?" A grizzled man with a long beard peered at them through the driver side window.

Was she? "Yes?"

"Is that a question or an answer?"

"An answer?" She set the suitcases in the truck bed and helped Karlie climb into the cab. "How far away from town are we?"

"From here? About half an hour. From a town big enough to give you a taste of city life, you'd have to drive forty-five minutes in the other direction."

Her eyes widened. The detective hadn't been kidding when he told her she'd be living in a remote location.

Half an hour up the mountain, they pulled in front of a rustic cabin. A porch extended along the front of it. A truck that appeared to be in better shape than the one they rode in sat out front. At least they'd have some mode of transportation.

"It's a good place. Roof don't leak. Well water is fresh and clear. A garden plot already hoed out back with seeds planted. Old man Rogers had everything ready before keeling over. Good luck."

"Thank you." Susan retrieved their suitcases and headed for the house.

Obviously locking the door wasn't a common

occurrence since the key was in the lock of the front door. "This is our new home, Karlie." She pushed open the door and stepped into a clean, comfortably furnished two-bedroom house.

No one could find them there.

Chapter One

Little did she know that what started as a normal day would end with a surprise that turns her world upside down.

"Bye, Mom." Karlie Marshall darted out the cabin door and rushed to her late model Toyota Tacoma. If she didn't hurry, she'd be late, again, for her shift as a waitress at Misty Hollow Diner. Her mom's words about being careful followed her across the yard.

Always the worrier, her mother. Quiet, content to work in her garden or fish the nearby lake, her mom stayed to herself, more than happy to sit at home when she wasn't working at the town's small library. Not Karlie. She loved her small town but wanted—no, needed—to visit a sprawling city. A place with more than the thirty thousand Shakerville had.

It almost wasn't worth the long drive just to buy something she couldn't find locally. Plus, whenever she mentioned leaving, her mother would almost have a heart attack. At twenty-five, it was past time for Karlie to make her own way. The problem was...she didn't know what she wanted. She loved Misty Hollow but craved a little more excitement than the small town had to offer.

The whoop whoop of a siren sounded behind her. Karlie glanced in her rearview mirror to see the blinking red and blue lights of a police car, then down at the speedometer. Ugh. Speeding again. She doubted she'd get away with a warning this time. She watched an officer approach in her side-view mirror. Not a familiar face. Was this the new sheriff everyone was talking about?

He tapped on the window. "License and registration, please."

Sighing, Karlie rolled down her window, then reached over to open the glove compartment. "I'm sorry, Sheriff. I was speeding. I'm late for work."

"Later now." His lips twitched. He took the documents and returned to his SUV.

Karlie leaned her head against the steering wheel. Idiot. She jerked upright as the sheriff returned. "You're new?"

"Sheriff Westbrook, at your service." He handed her back her documents, then a ticket.

"You're giving me a ticket?" Her voice rose.

"You were going fifteen miles over the speed limit, ma'am."

Her shoulders slumped. "Fine." She shoved the ticket into her purse. "Welcome to Misty Hollow." When he stepped back, she sped away, careful to only go five miles over the limit. She'd have to work overtime to pay for the ticket.

If she weren't so angry, and late, she'd dwell on how handsome the new sheriff was even with the reflective sunglasses he wore. Dark blond hair, chiseled chin with just a hint of a dimple. Too bad.

Darn. Her speed had crept up again.

She glanced in her rearview mirror. Was he following her? She slowed and took the turn into town.

"Sorry." She rushed to the back to put her purse in her locker. "I got pulled over for speeding."

"Bound to happen sooner or later with the way you drive." The owner, Myrtle McIlroy shook her head. "Maybe I should put you down for half an hour earlier every day so you'll arrive when you're actually supposed to."

Karlie laughed, then noticed her boss's new hair color. "Nice. Makes you look like Lucille Ball."

"Stop the flattery and get to work. We're already busy with the morning rush." She waved a dish towel in Karlie's direction. "The other girl called in sick. I've been busier than a one-armed paper hanger."

Karlie grabbed her apron and a menu as the bell over the diner door jingled. She rushed out and skid to a halt as the new sheriff entered. She swallowed when he smiled her way. "Just one?"

He nodded, removing his sunglasses to reveal hazel eyes. "Yes, ma'am."

"It's Karlie. Follow me, please." She led him to a booth. "I know cops like to be able to see all exits. Hope this will suffice."

"It will." He set his hat on the table and took his seat.

"Coffee?" Karlie handed him a menu.

"Please." The dimple in his cheek deepened.

"Newspaper?"

She left and returned with both, her gaze landing on the front page. "Who's Anthony Bartelloni?" She motioned to the story of a man being released from prison.

"Mob boss. He was released on probation. Should have stayed locked up for a very long time. I'll have the breakfast special."

Karlie placed the order and hurried to serve another customer, then glanced at the paper. The article said that Bartelloni had skipped out of town, left New York for parts unknown. She'd never heard the name before, but mobs were dangerous, right? She'd read about them in books.

"Table four's up," Myrtle called.

Karlie placed another order and carried the sheriff's food to him. "Let me know if you need anything else."

"How do you like Misty Hollow?"

"It's okay. A bit boring, and everyone knows everything about everyone else. Gossip is the favorite pastime." She smiled. "You arrived a couple of days ago, right?"

He nodded. "Looking forward to a slower pace."

"I'd say you've been busy already. Who tickets people before nine a.m.?" She arched a brow over flashing blue eyes, her smile fading. "Enjoy your breakfast." She marched away.

~

Yes, Heath had been busy. He knew exactly who Karlie Marshall was. Also knew who she used to be. With Bartelloni's whereabouts unknown, Heath had been filled in on the possible danger to Karlie and her

9

mother. The challenge would be keeping them safe without revealing their true identities. He was counting on the Misty Hollow gossip chain to let him know if any strangers arrived in town.

Karlie's laugh drew his attention to the pretty redhead. Imagine his surprise when he realized the identity of the woman he'd ticketed that morning. Heath hadn't expected to meet her so soon upon arriving in Misty Hollow. He'd been told that Sharon Marshall was a bit of a recluse and figured the daughter was as well.

Orders had been to make friends with the Marshall women. He wasn't off to a very good start. He read through the newspaper article. There wasn't much to go on. The FBI feared someone had leaked information about the women, but whether Bartelloni knew exactly where they were was unknown. So, erring on the side of caution, Heath went undercover as the new sheriff. He glanced out the window at the trees and vintage brick buildings. Staying here wouldn't be a hardship. It sure beat the concrete jungle of the city.

Breakfast finished, he left a hefty tip and headed to the register to pay for his meal and the paper. "Give the chef my compliments," he told Karlie.

"Myrtle, the sheriff said the food was good," she turned and called through the pass-thru window.

A middle-aged woman with bright orange hair popped up and grinned. "Thank you, Sheriff. Come again."

"I'll be a regular, most likely." He nodded and left, heading for his car. He'd been on the mountain to familiarize himself with the area around the Marshall home. Now, he intended to drive the other mountain roads to acquaint himself with empty places a man could hide. The area was so wooded sneaking up on a home would be easy.

His radio beeped. "Sheriff Westbrook."

"Sheriff, we've a call of a domestic situation on Coon Road," his receptionist, Annie, said.

"On my way." He punched the address into his GPS and sped toward the address.

A rundown trailer sat in the middle of what looked like a junkyard, but was more the result of hoarding. A pit bull barked and pulled against the chain holding him to a tree. Heath unclipped his gun holster, ready to shoot if the dog broke loose and charged. Loud voices came from inside the trailer. Heath beeped the horn and exited his SUV.

A man stepped onto a sagging porch. "What?"

"We've had a call about a disturbance."

"From who? We ain't got no neighbors." The man's stomach stretched the limits of a stained tee shirt.

"Is your wife home?"

"Sally, get your butt out here. The sheriff wants to talk to you."

A woman, as thin as the man was pudgy, joined him on the porch. "Shut up, Brute," she hollered at the dog. "I can't hear myself think." She crossed her arms. "What can I do for you, Sheriff?"

"Everything all right here?" He glanced from one to the other. Who'd called the sheriff's department? A hunter, maybe? The man was right. There were no neighbors within hearing distance.

"You might have to arrest me," she said. "I'm about to beat my husband's head in."

"Let's not do that. What's the problem?"

"She's mad because I sold some of her scrap metal to buy beer." The man rolled his eyes. "Look at this place. How'd she know anything was missing?"

How indeed? Heath warned them about keeping things civil and returned to his vehicle. If it had been a hunter who made the call, they were hunting illegally. His day just got busier. He drove down a little-used path called a road and parked next to Misty Hollow Lake. A red-haired woman fished from the bank. Sharon Marshall.

She turned as he cut off the engine. "Howdy, Sheriff."

"Ma'am. Did you place a call to the station about a disturbance?"

"Yes. They were disturbing the peace, and I feared someone would be injured." Worry crossed the woman who looked like an older version of Karlie.

"Just an argument. Getting any bites?"

She bent over and lifted a string from the water. "Three bass. Enough for supper."

He wanted to warn her not to go out alone. To stay home. But, without solid proof that Bartelloni knew where she was, making her afraid seemed wrong.

"Why don't you come by for supper?" She smiled. "There'll be plenty." She gave him her address. "It's always nice to make friends with the local authorities."

Smart woman. Making friends meant local law enforcement would keep a closer eye on their friend. Would she change her mind when she heard he'd ticketed her daughter? "I'd love to. See you later, ma'am."

By the end of his workday, Heath looked forward to a home-cooked meal. Eating out became old after a while, and he wanted a chance to see the Marshalls in their home. Determine, if possible, how defenseless they might be.

He changed into jeans and a button-up shirt, shoved his feet into cowboy boots, packed his things and then checked out of the motel. He climbed into his SUV, radio clipped to his belt. He might be officially off work, but his job never really ended at five o'clock. Not in such a small town where the station held him and two others.

Heath pulled into the graveled drive of the Marshall place and studied the cleared lawn. As with most of the homes out of the town limits, woods surrounded the house on three sides. Someone had cleared a nice space for a lawn and a garden. But this place gave a new meaning to the word, remote. A good thing when in the Witness Protection program. Bad if someone you'd wronged wanted to get to you—

On the porch, he raised his hand to knock and stopped as Karlie's voice rose inside.

"Mom, why does the DNA test I got back today show that I'm the daughter of Anthony Bartelloni?"

Chapter Two

It had to be a mistake. "Someone goofed, right?" Karlie read the results again, an ache forming in the back of her throat at the paleness of her mother's face. "Mom?"

"Why'd you have to take that test? Couldn't you leave well enough alone?"

"I wanted to know more about my father." Maybe not this much.

Her mother opened and closed her mouth several times. Tears filled her eyes. "I'll explain."

A knock sounded at the door. A visible look of relief crossed her mother's face. "Later. The sheriff is here for supper."

"What?" Karlie frowned. "Why?"

"I thought it best we make friends. Now, it seems even more important that he's on our side."

"Did you see the paper? Bartelloni is out on probation and skipped out of New York. Mom, this is not good."

Her mother reached a trembling hand toward the door handle. "No more. We'll talk later." She opened the door. "Good evening, Sheriff Westbrook."

"Please call me Heath." He glanced at Karlie.

The look in his eyes told her everything she needed to know. "You know?"

He nodded. "I'll explain."

Karlie rolled her eyes. "Great. Both of you have secrets. Why not talk at once? Fill me in on the lie my life has been." She tossed the DNA results on the table. All her life she'd dreamed of who her father might be. The soldier who died while deployed—at least that's the story Mom had told her. The recurrent dreams of riding on a bus, being called Kayla, playmates…that *was* the truth. Not the last twenty years in this cabin. Well, she craved excitement. Looks like she'd get it.

"Come eat." Head down, shoulders slumped, her mother turned toward the kitchen.

Karlie doubted she'd have an appetite. She shot a glare at Heath and followed her mother to help carry the dishes to the table—catfish, green beans, and hushpuppies. "Were you married to him?"

"Yes, but I never took his name. For some insane reason, he thought it best. Maybe it was a vain attempt to protect me. Who knows?" Mom set a plate in front of Heath, then one in front of Karlie. "Before I start talking, I'd like to know what the sheriff knows."

"Call me Heath, please. We'll be seeing a lot of each other." He set down the fork he'd just picked up. "I'm actually FBI. The instant Bartelloni left New York, I was assigned the vacant sheriff's position as undercover to watch over the two of you. My suggestion is that you move again, change your names—"

"No." Karlie shook her head. "Absolutely not. I've spent the last twenty years in hiding, which I didn't even know about until just now. I doubt my biological father will kill me. If he even finds me."

"He'll find you. Have no doubt about that. He has eyes and ears everywhere. No, he might not kill you, but he will kill your mother for betraying him." Heath's words and the hard glint in his eyes stabbed Karlie's heart.

"Mom?"

"I thought I'd fallen in love with a rich man who did good things in the community. I went with him when he did his charity work. That's not all he was doing. It wasn't until you turned five that I overheard Anthony ordering a hit on a rival mob boss. Then, all the secret conversations behind doors made sense. Until then, I'd been nothing but a pretty woman hanging on his arm, enjoying the life of luxury he gave me.

"When the news broke of the brutal murder of the man whose name I'd heard mentioned, I broke into Anthony's office, stole his files, and met with the state prosecutor. They put us into Witness Protection, and we fled. That's it."

"I'm not running again." Karlie hung her head. "You can, but I'm staying for whatever comes."

"Anthony Bartelloni isn't a man to trifle with," Heath said. "If he doesn't trust you, he'll kill you."

"I'm probably the only one who can keep him from killing my mother." She stared at the breaded fish in front of her, then pushed her plate away. How had such an ordinary day become anything but?

"Bartelloni is unpredictable, as your mother can

tell you." Heath shook his head. "He won't play games. You're his only child. He'll do whatever it takes to take you back to New York. Once there, you'll be forced into his lifestyle, forced to marry one of his top henchmen. Is that what you want?"

"No." An icy fist clenched her heart. "We'll leave our safety in your hands, but I'm not running again. I need some fresh air." Karlie doubted danger had arrived yet, unless she counted the new undercover sheriff as dangerous. His arrival definitely meant trouble for Misty Hollow and the Marshalls.

She rushed out the front door and sat on the porch swing, setting it into motion with her big toe. Her gaze roamed the thickening shadows of the woods. Would danger come from the mountain or drive brazenly up the road? Let it come. She'd grown up country, knew how to hunt, could shoot a squirrel out of a tree with a bow and arrow. Her father didn't have a clue what he'd face if he came for her or her mother.

~

"You hold too many secrets, Ms. Marshall."

Sharon glanced at the sheriff. "There can never be too many when it comes to protecting your daughter."

His expression said he didn't agree. "Once she became an adult, you could have told her rather than her finding out this way."

"I never intended for her to find out." She clutched her hands together tight enough to turn her knuckles white.

"Things have been set into motion that cannot be undone." He stormed from the room, mumbling something about his job being harder now.

Sharon bit the inside of her cheek to prevent the

tears from flowing. All her hard work, all the dangers she'd kept at bay, had risen up like a bird from the ashes and threatened to engulf Karlie in flames.

She stood and moved to the window and stared at the woods behind the house. The place had always brought her calm. Now the deepening shadows cast a cloud of doom. They were no longer safe in Misty Hollow.

~

Karlie did not look pleased, or surprised, to see Heath join her on the porch. "May I?" He motioned to a chair.

"It's a free country."

Holding back a sigh, Heath lowered himself into the wooden chair. "I'm sorry this is happening. I promise to do my best to keep you and your mother safe. Don't shoot me, but I'll be living on your sofa for a while."

Her eyes widened. "How will that look to the town, the new sheriff living here?"

"I'm staying with friends until I get my own place. That's all anyone needs to know."

"Friends." She smirked. "You gave me a ticket for speeding, remember?"

"Because you were speeding." He grinned, trying to lighten the mood.

She sighed and stared over his shoulder. "I'm getting a dog. A big one."

"Good idea."

"I also know how to shoot."

"Good to know."

Her sharp gaze trained back on him. "I'm no wilting violet."

"I can see that." He laughed. "Let's work together, okay? I'm on your side."

She shrugged. "What's your plan?"

"We wait until we know where your father is."

"Don't call him that. I don't have a father." She lunged to her feet and stormed across the lawn, leaving Heath to follow.

"You shouldn't go anywhere alone."

"You're here, aren't you?" She stopped on the edge of a small pond across the road. "This is one of my favorite places. I used to come here and dream of who my father was, what my life would be like if he hadn't died." She bent and picked up a rock, skipping it across the water. "Now, I've been told he's very much alive and probably the least person anyone would want to be fathered by."

Heath skipped a rock after hers. "I'm sorry you were deceived. It was for your and your mother's safety. Sharon did what she thought was right. Could you live a life of crime had you known?"

"No." Her second rock went farther than the first. She gave a sardonic laugh. "Just this morning, I wished for excitement in my life. Be careful what you wish for, right?"

He nodded. "I'll get my things out of my car." After glancing around the area and not seeing anything of the ordinary, he left her at the water's edge and retrieved his things.

"So, you really are staying." Sharon turned from the mantel, a gun in her hand. On the weathered beam that served as the fireplace mantel sat an opened ornate box. She arched a brow. "Just in case this day came, I learned to shoot a long time ago."

"Karlie says she's a good shot as well."

"She is. I wanted both of us to be prepared, and we hunt like most of the locals do, so all of our target practice didn't raise any suspicions." She closed the box and set the gun on top. "This isn't the only gun in the house. I've got one in every room."

"I'll need to know where they are." He dropped his bag on the floor.

"I'd offer to bunk with my daughter, but she's angry with me." Sharon managed a weak smile.

"The sofa is fine. Hopefully, it won't be for long." Heath was glad to know the woman had prepared for such a time. He doubted he could keep the two safe on his own. "Since I am acting sheriff, I'll have to do my job in addition to keeping you safe. You'll have to continue living as if nothing is wrong. It'll be dangerous. Always have a weapon with you."

"I'm ready." She slouched on the sofa. "Karlie will cooperate. Once she's over the shock of knowing her entire life has been a lie, she'll come around."

Heath hoped so. The last thing any of them needed was for Karlie to go out on her own to find Bartelloni. "She won't go all vigilante, will she?"

"Lord, I hope not. My daughter is headstrong, but she isn't stupid." She got to her feet. "I'll fetch you some blankets."

Heath moved to the front window, barely able to make out Karlie's silhouette by the pond. He didn't like her out alone, not even in her front yard, but making her feel stifled would drive her to do something drastic.

He watched as she turned and strolled back to the house, head up, shoulders back as if she'd come to an acceptance of her situation. He opened the door for her, then engaged the deadbolt. "You going to be all right?"

Her gaze landed on the gun resting on the mantel. "Yes. Looks like Mom is getting prepared to do battle."

"There won't be a peaceful ending to this."

"I don't expect there will. Can I still go to work? We need the money."

"Yes, life will go on as normal, but exercise caution, and pack a gun."

She crossed her arms. "I want everything you have on my father."

"Okay. I have files on my laptop. What's your email?" He pulled his computer from his bag and opened it on the coffee table. When she gave him her email address, he sent the files. "He isn't a good man."

"I wouldn't expect a mob boss to be good. Good night, Sheriff."

"Heath," he muttered as she left the room. He sure hoped she wouldn't be this prickly all the time. He understood her anger, but they needed cool heads until Bartelloni was behind bars again.

"Here you go." Sharon placed blankets and a pillow on the edge of the sofa. "It's a pullout and not too uncomfortable."

"I'll be fine."

"Where's Karlie?"

"In her room learning about her father." He closed his laptop and sat back. "It's best she knows everything about him."

"I agree. Good night, Heath. Thank you for being here."

He sure hoped he didn't regret accepting the assignment. After pulling out the bed and making it, he went to the bathroom to change into cotton lounge pants before stretching out on what would be his bed for who knew how many nights.

Arms folded behind his head, he stared at the ceiling. Misty Hollow, a quaint small town right out of a Norman Rockwell painting. But evil was coming to this town. Heath prayed Misty Hollow could handle Bartelloni and his men. He prayed he could handle the task in front of him.

Chapter Three

Karlie set her purse in her locker with a thump. She hated carrying a gun. Besides, if anyone came for her in the diner, she'd never reach her weapon in time.

She'd stayed up far too late the night before reading about one of the most vile beings God had ever created. To think he was her father left a sour taste in her mouth.

"You're out of sorts this morning," Myrtle said, "but you are on time, so I won't complain."

"Sheriff Westbrook drove me in. Turns out, he's a friend of my mother's and is staying with us for a while."

Myrtle grinned. "Not much of a hardship. That man is easy on the eyes."

Karlie agreed but only nodded as she tied on her apron. "Our cabin is too small for three people."

"Makes it even better." The other woman wiggled

her eyebrows. "Close confinement."

Karlie smiled, despite her sullen mood. Best to accept the situation and move on. Her mother had also been dropped off at work with orders not to leave the library until Heath picked her up later. Maybe things would be okay after all.

When she entered the eating area, Heath had chosen to sit in the same spot as yesterday, only this time he hadn't removed his hat. Karlie followed his narrowed-eyed gaze to where two men she didn't recognize sat a couple of booths away. With a motion of his head, Heath made it clear he wanted her to wait on them.

Fine. It wasn't her table, but the other waitress was busy. Karlie would make sure the tip went to the proper person. "Good morning, I'm Karlie. Can I get either of you coffee?"

The two men nodded, both wearing new jeans and flannel shirts with the creases still showing. Either tourists or newcomers trying to fit in. The problem with their attire was the heat index would rise to close to a hundred by the afternoon.

Karlie smiled and went to pour their coffee, letting Annie know she was helping with her section until hers got busy.

"Thank you. I'm not feeling well this morning and moving slow." She swiped a hand across her brow. "I may go home after the morning rush." Her blue eyes looked pained, her light red hair pulled back too tight from her pale face.

"Go sit down. I've got this." Karlie grabbed the coffeepot and some packets of cream and sugar, then returned to the table. "Have you decided?"

"We'll both have the pancake special," the older man said.

"Are you visiting or new to our town?" Karlie filled their cups.

"Visiting," he said with a thick New York accent. "What is there to do around here?"

"It isn't hunting season, other than squirrel, so mostly hiking, fishing, or visiting thrift shops and antique stores. We have plenty of those." She kept a smile on her face, despite the hard look in the man's eyes.

"What's wrong with the other gal? She's the one who seated us."

"Annie isn't feeling well. Don't worry. I'll take good care of you."

A prickly sensation crawled up her arms. The man's smile looked forced, his gaze continuing to drift to where Annie sat alone in a booth, nursing a glass of orange juice. When she slumped over, Karlie rushed to her side.

"Annie?" The woman's eyes were closed. Seconds later, Heath was at Karlie's side.

He felt for a pulse. "Call an ambulance." He knelt next to Annie and patted her face. "What's her name?"

"Annie Jones." Karlie darted for the phone.

The two men watched with interest over the happenings, their heads close together in conversation. A strange pair.

Assured an ambulance would arrive in minutes, Karlie ducked into the kitchen long enough to place the men's orders and let Myrtle know Annie had collapsed. Then, she returned to Heath. "She'd complained about not feeling well a few minutes ago. Can you tell what's wrong?"

He sniffed the orange juice. "Does this smell funny to you?"

She sniffed the juice. "It smells old. That's impossible, though. Myrtle is very careful about tossing out anything expired or left out. No one goes in the kitchen without her approval."

"Hmm. Has she worked here long?"

"Longer than I have." She started to ask what he was thinking, but the wail of sirens, then the arrival of two paramedics had her returning to her job. Poor Annie. Karlie hoped she'd be okay. "Let me grab her purse from the back."

She rushed to the storage room at the far end of the kitchen and grabbed Annie's purse and water bottle before returning to Heath.

He glanced at the water bottle, his face setting in grim lines. "Do you know whether she goes anywhere before coming to work?"

"No." She picked up the two men's orders, plunked the plates on the table, and rushed to wait on another customer, stopping at the sound of snapping fingers. She turned back to the table she'd just left. "Yes?"

"Does this happen often?" The younger man asked. "Is it food poisoning?"

Karlie pasted on what she hoped was a reassuring smile. "Nothing to worry about. Most likely a stomach bug. The food is safe to eat." The older man didn't seem to have the same worries as his companion since he was already digging in. "Enjoy your stay in Misty Hollow."

Work and conversation in the diner ceased as

Annie was placed on a stretcher and wheeled from the building. Karlie met Heath's worried gaze.

"Don't leave the diner without me," he whispered, as he followed the paramedic out. "I'll be back as soon as I know how Annie is."

~

The moment Heath and Karlie left, Sharon grabbed her rifle from the pantry and headed into the woods. There were a lot of places a body could hide. It would take her days, weeks, to check them all out.

Bartelloni's men could be hiding in one of the caves waiting to catch them unaware. But, not if she found them first.

The packed dirt and moss-covered ground muffled her footsteps. She'd hiked the woods enough not to make a sound when she walked. Avoiding the path Karlie always took to her favorite lookout, Sharon headed up the mountain rather than the easier way around.

Did she still have secrets untold? Of course. She'd have to be careful to keep them hidden.

Ahead of her loomed the tree with a hole about head-high. She stuck her hand inside and pulled out a small weatherproof pouch. She knew the perfect hiding place.

~

Heath followed the ambulance to the hospital, then the doctor to Annie's room. "I want her tested for poison and drugs." He'd already called for one of the other officers to collect the glass of orange juice from his car. Annie looked enough like a child-version of Karlie that Heath wasn't ignoring the possibility of foul play.

The doctor assured him they'd check into both, and if the sheriff didn't mind waiting in the waiting room, he'd be with him as soon as he knew something. Heath nodded and returned to a small room set aside for family.

As he waited, he thought of the two strangers in town. Men too stupid to know how badly they stuck out among the locals. He stood when the doctor entered the room a few hours later.

"Miss Jones had a very strong drug in her system. One meant to knock her out, not kill her. She had a bad reaction. It's a good thing she took the drug while people were around."

Heath strongly doubted she took the drug by choice. "Thank you. Please keep me informed on her condition." He left and headed for the police station.

Officer Baines had night duty that week so he'd left it up to the rookie, Officer Wood, to get the orange juice and water to the lab. "The doctor confirmed she was drugged, but I'd like the lab to confirm and let us know if there was anything else in that juice or water. She could have been poisoned before reaching the diner if she made a stop."

"This is a peaceful town, Sheriff. Why would someone want to harm a gal as sweet as Annie?"

"Trouble is coming. Word is that Bartelloni and his men might have their sights on Misty Hollow." Heath flipped through his messages.

"Why here? This is small-town country."

Heath didn't want to lie, but the less anyone knew about the Marshall family the better. "Expansion? Hiding in plain sight?" He shrugged. "All I know is the warning I received from the FBI said to be on the lookout."

"But why Annie?" Officer Wood's brow furrowed. "Do you think she saw or heard something?"

"We'll know when she's conscious." Heath doubted it. His gut told him they thought she was Karlie and drugged her so they could abduct her and turn her over to Bartelloni. "I want a guard placed on Miss Jones's hotel room asap. You can do it until help arrives."

"Got it." The officer strode from the building.

Heath had done all he could for the time being to keep the residents of Misty Hollow safe. Last night, he'd asked the FBI for more undercover agents in town. They'd promised to send some officers from St. Louis. Hopefully, they'd arrive in time.

At noon, Heath headed back to the diner and sat in his usual booth. Karlie fluttered from one customer to the next like a hummingbird. Fatigue clouded her pretty features, but her smile stayed in place. When a lull came in the rush, she slid into the seat across from Heath.

"How's Annie? I've been worried about her all morning." She folded her hands on the tabletop and took a deep breath.

"Someone gave her a drug that should have knocked her out, not almost kill her. Tell me your opinion of the two men in the flannel shirts." Heath leaned back in his seat. "I know you don't have much time, so whatever you can give me, I'll take."

"They didn't fit in. The clothes were too new and unfit for the season. They looked anything but like a couple of country boys. Plus, their New York accent was so thick it was almost hard to understand."

"Here's what I think. I believe they were sent here to get you. Consider this...Annie looks like what you would have looked like as a child, right? Was your hair lighter?"

She paled. "You might be onto something. When we go home later, there are some pictures of me in the attic. It might be time to drag them out."

"It could be confirmation at least."

"Gotta go. See you at five. We have a lunch special today." She slid from the booth. "Bacon cheeseburger."

"I'll take it." He grinned as she rushed off. At least she seemed to be thinking clearer today, although he wasn't sure how she'd respond if she'd been the target and not Annie. He needed to find out how the drug had been added to Annie's juice.

After lunch, he returned to the hospital. Annie's room was in chaos.

"What's going on?" He stopped a harried nurse.

"Your officer was attacked, and Miss Jones has vanished from her room." She darted away.

Heath sprinted to the room where Annie had been admitted. Her bed was empty. On the other bed lay a groggy Officer Baines.

"What happened?" Heath plopped into the chair next to the bed.

"I went to the bathroom. A nurse agreed to stay here until I returned. She was checking vitals. When I came back and stepped into the room, someone hit me in the back of the head. When I came to, Annie was gone."

"What nurse? Would you recognize her again?"

He nodded. "Help me up. I'll take a look around."

Heath helped him to his feet and supported him to

the door. Baines glanced toward the nurse's station. "I don't see her."

"Nametag?"

"Lana"

Heath glanced at the board listing which nurse was on duty to care for Annie. "No Lana." He flagged down another nurse. "I'd like to speak to a nurse named Lana."

"We don't have a nurse by that name."

"No one saw an imposter enter this room?"

"Sir, we've had a busy day. Anyone could have entered if dressed appropriately."

"Put out a BOLO on Annie Jones," Heath said into his radio. "Early twenties, light red hair, blue eyes, and wearing a hospital gown."

He helped Baines back to the bed. "Take it easy. Don't rush out of here. It won't locate Annie." Nope, she was probably on her way to New York by now, and they'd most likely never find out how she got the poison.

What would Bartelloni do to her when he discovered he had the wrong woman?

Chapter Four

Karlie woke the next morning, her heart heavy. Annie had been abducted in her place. Bartelloni didn't sound like the kind of man to let her go after finding out the mistake.

She swung her legs over the side of the bed. Going to the diner, listening to speculation as to Annie's whereabouts, was not something she relished. She'd have to bite her tongue to keep from revealing either hers or Heath's true identities.

As she moved past the living room, Heath shot to a sitting position and reached for the gun on the coffee table. He blinked at her a few times before speaking, "Sorry. I'm a bit on edge."

"Did you find out anything about Annie?"

He shook his head. "In this case, no news is good news."

She frowned. "You look like you could use some

coffee."

"Most definitely." He tossed off the thin sheet he wore.

Wrenching her gaze away from the chiseled chest and cotton shorts sitting low on his hips, Karlie stepped into the kitchen. The last thing she needed right now was a relationship, especially with a man undercover. Once Bartelloni was caught, Heath would be gone.

Her mother sat at the small table, staring into the cup in her hands as if the weight of the world rested on her shoulders. More secrets or just the severity of their situation?

"Are you okay?" Karlie pulled two more mugs from the cabinet.

"Heath told me about the other waitress being taken." She glanced up. "I'm so glad your hair darkened as you grew, despite your dislike of the color for a while. It kept you safe, at least for now."

She poured coffee, added flavored cream to hers and turned. "I'm scared for Annie. She doesn't deserve this."

"Hopefully. If Bartelloni believes her denials, he'll have her killed." Mom pushed to her feet. "I'd better get dressed. Can't go to work in my nightgown." Her shoulders remained slumped as if weighted down.

Maybe they were. Fear and worry could weigh on a person. In fact, Karlie's limbs felt coated with cement. She shuffled to the living room. Heath must have gone to get dressed. She set his mug on the table and headed to her room to put on her uniform.

Half an hour later, Heath dropped her mother off at the library and entered the diner with Karlie. "Looks like breakfast is a daily occurrence here for me," he said.

"You could eat in worse places." She smiled and headed for the back to lock up her things.

"No Annie again today?" Myrtle glanced up from the stove.

"Guess not."

"She must be really sick."

Karlie nodded and grabbed her pad and pencil before leaving to take orders. The two strangers from the night before were absent. Another sign that they might be responsible for Annie's drugging.

As she'd suspected, Heath ordered the morning's special, pancakes this time with a side of bacon. Other customers ordered the same, keeping Myrtle's griddle busy.

Karlie leaned on the counter between customers and stared out the large front window which showcased a bookstore and an antique store across the street. How could such a picturesque town be the center of evil and danger? Could Misty Hollow handle what was coming? Could she?

Heath raised a hand to motion her over. She grabbed the coffeepot and headed to refill his cup.

"Try not to worry too much," he told her. "Hopefully, we've a few days of respite before Annie's identity is discovered. When she says she isn't you, Bartelloni will have someone check out her story."

"Do you think she can survive this?"

"I hope so. The FBI in New York is looking out for her. If they can save her, they will."

Then that's what Karlie would hope for. Extraction and safety for Annie who would then most likely go into witness protection herself unless Bartelloni was taken down along with his minions. If not, they'd all be looking over their shoulders for a very long time.

The bell over the door jingled, pulling her to greet the new arrivals. A middle-aged man and woman asked to be seated at a booth. "Welcome to Misty Hollow Diner." Karlie handed them menus. "Is this your first time here?"

"Oh, yes, dear." The woman's thick Southern drawl spilled over like warm gravy. "We're looking to settle down here. Small town life has always called to us. I'm Betty Snallings, and this is my husband, Ted."

"Welcome. I'm sure you'll enjoy it here. There are a few homes for sale but mainly outside of the town limits." Karlie smiled and promised to return with glasses of water.

"We've met with the local realtor." Ted's response followed her to the kitchen.

"If Annie doesn't come back soon," Myrtle said, "we're going to have to hire help. You can't work all day every day."

"Maybe you can hire someone temporarily. Then, if Annie doesn't return, they can go full-time."

Myrtle's eyes widened. "Why wouldn't she come back? What have you heard?"

Karlie licked her suddenly dry lips. "Nothing really," she lied, "but she's mentioned moving back home."

"I'd think a girl like Annie would give me notice."

"Maybe since she took sick, she decided to go back to her parents' place." Karlie shrugged and rushed out to take the Snallings' orders. She'd almost messed up big time and said far too much.

~

35

After hearing a report on his radio, Heath raced back to the diner and to Karlie. "Can you get away? The library is on fire."

She whirled to face Myrtle. "I—"

"Go. We're between rushes. I'll manage. Hopefully, you can be back by the lunch rush. I'll call in my niece. She hates working here but will help me out in a pinch." She waved Karlie away. "Sharon is more important."

"What do you know?" Karlie said, sliding into Heath's squad car.

"Only that it's on fire."

"Any word on my mother?"

Heath shook his head. "No one has seen her." He reached over and squeezed Karlie's hand. "Don't worry. She has to gotten out." He hoped Sharon was somewhere safe watching the fire. Heath turned on the sirens and sped to the library. Flames licked one side of the building, slowed by the brick walls. Fire trucks had arrived, and a large crowd gathered across the street. Shoving open his door, he approached one of the firemen. "Any sign of the librarian?"

"We've gotten everyone out as far as we know."

"She would be in her office," Karlie said, gripping the man's arm. "Did you check?"

When the fireman responded that he didn't know, Heath sprinted for the library.

"Hey, you can't go in there," a man called out.

Pounding of feet told Heath that Karlie was right behind him. "Do not leave my side," he told her. "Show me to the office."

She darted through the open door and turned right. "Mom?"

In a far corner of the building was a closed door with an office plaque hanging on the outside. Heath turned the handle. Locked. "Stand back." He placed a well-aimed kick, then another, until the door slammed open. The room was empty.

His heart dropped to his knees. "The bathroom."

Changing direction, her apron pulled up over her nose, Karlie led the way down a hall to a room labeled Women. "Mom?"

A cough from the far stall urged Heath on. He opened the door to see Sharon slumped on the floor. "Help me get her up." He drew one of her arms around his shoulders, letting Karlie do the same on the other side.

Two firemen met them when they stepped back into the hall. "Who didn't check the bathroom?" One of them asked. "Find out. This woman could have died."

Heath would like to wring the neck of whoever didn't check thoroughly. By now, his throat burned from the thickening smoke, and he choked back a cough.

Outside, he turned Sharon over to the firemen and bent over, placing his hands on his knees as he took gulps of fresh air. Karlie, having used her apron, seemed to have fared better and followed after her mother.

Within seconds, an oxygen mask was placed over Sharon's nose and mouth. She pulled the mask away when Heath stepped beside her. "I don't think it was Bartelloni."

"Why do you say that?"

"Because I ran some kids off who were setting off smoke bombs in the men's room. Think it was an accident. I went to the bathroom to…well, have a good cry, then I succumbed to the smoke." She replaced the mask over her face.

They'd find out soon enough. The fire marshal would know whether the fire was set deliberately.

"Go back to work, Karlie," Sharon said. "I'm fine."

"You could have died." Tears shimmered in Karlie's eyes.

"But I didn't. Go on. I'll have work to do here once the fire is out."

Already the flames were being extinguished. Only one wall and part of the roof were destroyed, but the damage to the books would be huge.

Heath took Karlie's arm. "Come on. You're needed elsewhere."

"Mom isn't safe here alone."

"She's safe with the firemen. I'll have one of the other officers come stay with her and bring her to the diner when she's done here."

Karlie nodded reluctantly. "I want to know at once if the fire was set deliberately." She pulled free of his grasp and marched to the car.

"I promise you'll know as soon as I know." With the danger to the Marshall women increasing, he wouldn't hold back anything to help keep them safe. He dropped Karlie off at the diner and returned to the police station. Heath wanted to check out the new couple in town—the Snallings, he'd heard them say. From this point forward, he'd run a background check on every newcomer. He already had people working on the town's residents. If there were any more imposters, he'd flush them out. Hopefully, before anyone else was harmed.

"Officer Baines, I need you to go to the library and watch over Mrs. Marshall. Take her to the diner when she's finished there."

"Yes, sir." The officer rushed from the building.

Heath flipped through his messages, saw nothing that warranted his immediate attention, and sat down at his computer to see what he could dig up on the new couple. After a couple of hours, he didn't see anything to raise any red flags. They seemed clean, the man a retired postal worker, three adult children who lived in Savannah. Once the couple was settled, he'd head to their place and introduce himself.

His phone rang. "Sheriff Westbrook."

"Fire Chief Morrison. The fire at the library seems to have been started by a smoke bomb in a trashcan behind the nonfiction section of the library." He gave Heath the names of the boys Sharon had run off. "Accident most likely, but you might want to check it out."

"I sure do." Heath hung up and headed to a small housing development on the outskirts of town.

Two of the boys were brothers, the other a neighbor. He found them running down the side of the road and pulled up beside them with a squawk of his siren. "Stop right there, boys. You've got some explaining to do."

"We didn't mean to do anything wrong." The oldest boy crossed his arms.

"You don't think setting off smoke bombs in the library was wrong? You started a fire." Heath climbed out and opened the back door. "Get in. We'll have to call your parents. They aren't going to be happy to have to pay for the damage you caused."

This type of work seemed like a cakewalk after dealing with the Bartelloni gang. Maybe when things were all over, he'd remain the sheriff of Misty Hollow. He might live longer.

~

A cry to release tension had been long overdue. Giving into emotions she rarely let herself experience had almost gotten Sharon killed. When she'd smelled the smoke, her first thought had been that she would die next to the toilet, but reason returned and reminded her of the pranks the boys had pulled.

Now, she waited at home, anxious for Karlie to return. Anxiety—that was a familiar emotion lately. Fear clogged her throat at the fact that one day, five o'clock would come with no sign of her daughter. The day would come when Karlie would be back in her father's clutches.

Would Sharon have the courage to face Bartelloni and get her back? She stood and paced the living room. Just the thought of seeing him again made her blood run cold. Once, he'd claimed she was his queen. If she went back, she'd become his slave. Sharon preferred death.

Parting the curtains on the front window, she stared at the afternoon sun glinting off the lake's surface. Not even the gorgeous view could release the tension tightening inside her. Nothing would except seeing Karlie's face when she walked through the front door.

Chapter Five

Her first day off in a while. Karlie laced up her hiking boots, ready to walk off some stress. The diner had hired another girl when it became apparent to Myrtle that Annie wouldn't return, lessening Karlie's workload. She needed this day.

She opened her bedroom door to see Heath standing there, his hand raised to knock. The look on his face had her taking a step back. "What is it?"

"Annie's body was found in Central Park. Someone slit her throat."

A sob escaped. "That poor girl. She didn't deserve it."

"Nor do you," he said.

"So, Bartelloni must have discovered she wasn't me." Which meant he'd still be looking for her. Poor Annie, killed because she looked like her. It was her fault Annie died. She scrubbed a hand over her cheek.

Lines formed around Heath's lips. "The danger to you and your mother has increased. I think it best the two of you take a leave of absence from your jobs."

"Absolutely not." She brushed past him. "We'll be on our guard, but I refuse to live in fear." Brave words despite the ice water running through her veins.

He reached out and grabbed her arm, turning her to face him. "Please, listen to reason, Karlie. This cabin is far safer than in town. We can set up a warning perimeter. Bartelloni has proven he will kill innocent people in order to get to you."

She yanked her arm free. "Are you going to take a leave of absence?"

"No, I'm the acting sheriff, undercover or not."

"And I have a job to do. It wouldn't be fair to the diner." She marched to the kitchen and started preparing a sack lunch.

"Where are you going?"

"Hiking. It's how I work off steam. I've two places to go, the mountain and the lake. Today, I choose the mountain."

"Guess I'll put my hiking shoes on. You aren't going alone."

She arched a brow. "What about your job?"

"I'll have the others fill in, and I'll take the night shift. They can radio me if there's trouble."

There would be no arguing with the man. "Take Mom to work first, then I'll be ready to go."

He narrowed his eyes. "You plan on leaving without me."

"No…" She didn't sound convincing even to her ears.

"You two stop arguing." Mom entered the room, shaking her head. "The library is closed until the fire damage is repaired. I'll be off work for weeks and staying home alone isn't new to me."

Heath grinned. "Problem solved." He turned and left to put on his shoes.

By the time Karlie had lunch and water bottles prepared, he returned in khaki shorts which showcased muscled legs, hiking boots, and a tee shirt that emphasized his chest and arms. The man looked too good for anyone's sanity. She handed him his bag and a water bottle, then placed hers into a lightweight backpack. "Let's get started before the day becomes too hot."

"Lead the way." He slung a backpack over his shoulder. "I'll try to keep up."

She rolled her eyes, knowing he could leave her in the dust if he wanted to. "Be careful, Mom."

"I plan on doing some fishing, laundry, reading…and I'll be just fine." She patted the gun on her hip. "Got my friend right here."

"How do you feel about a dog?"

"That sounds like a good idea. You and Heath can adopt one after your hike. A big dog."

Karlie laughed. "I'll see what I can find."

"I have an idea," Heath said. "A friend of mine in the area keeps retired police and military dogs. I can give him a call and have a dog here by this afternoon." He pulled out his cell phone and sent a text.

"Even better." Karlie smiled. "A dog already trained." She led the way out the back door and into the woods. The only destination she had in mind was a bluff overlooking a valley. The scenery calmed her and made the perfect place to eat lunch.

"I'm not trying to be heavy-handed," Heath said, falling into step beside her. "I only want to keep you and your mother safe. It's my job."

Right. His job. "I get it, and you know my stand on this." She moved aside a low-hanging branch. The thick tree cover kept the sun from bearing down on them. "If we don't take a stand, Bartelloni will never stop."

"You could die."

"Then I was meant to. Believe me, I don't intend to go down quietly." She didn't intend to die at all.

They fell into a comfortable silence, Karlie's favorite way to hike. Rather than conversation, she preferred the sound of the wind in the trees and the birds' songs. She stopped as a doe stepped onto the path a few yards ahead of them. The animal's ears stiffened, she stared at them for a few seconds, then continued on her way.

"Beautiful," Heath whispered.

"Yes, but I would have shot her during season. Oh." Two fawns followed the path their mother took. "That's why there is a hunting season. The babies need their mother for a while."

"You and your mother must be close having lived so long with just the two of you."

"We are. I was angry at the secrets she kept from me, but I see her point now that I've had time to think about it. She did what she needed to in order to keep me from a life of crime. My father would have wanted me to marry someone to take over his so-called business." That would have been a fate worse than death. Or, maybe, she would have been so used to that lifestyle she would have followed orders without argument.

What would she say to him when they came face-to-face? "What if, when he comes, I agree to go with him? With someone on the inside, you could gain information about his dealings that you wouldn't be able to otherwise."

"If you were found out, you'd end up like Annie. We wouldn't be able to protect you."

"I'd protect myself." She stopped at the bluff. "Here's where I always stop to have lunch. Isn't the view amazing?"

She stepped to the edge and gazed over a sea of green. A faint sheen hovered over the trees if one arrived there early enough to witness it, thus giving the town its name. In the distance, the blue ribbon of a river snaked through the foliage. "If a person were to paint this, it wouldn't look the same."

Heath moved to her side. "No, it wouldn't. It is truly beautiful." Only his gaze rested on her and not on the view.

~

Heath enjoyed the flush of color in Karlie's cheeks when she'd caught him staring at her. Smiling, he sat cross-legged on the bluff and pulled his lunch from his pack. "Tell me about growing up? What do you remember about your time before Misty Hollow?"

"I remember Mom saying we were going on an adventure. We rode a bus here, and I clutched a stuffed bunny like a lifeline. It was a lot of change for a child of five. Wonder what happened to that bunny? Maybe it's in the attic. I'll check when I have time. It disappeared one day shortly after we arrived, although I don't know why Mom would have taken it from me." She unwrapped her sandwich.

"How was it living here in the woods?"

"It didn't take long for me to adjust. I loved the trees and the water. I could run wild in my front yard, swim in the lake, watch squirrels and rabbits chase each other, which I thought was magical after the concrete of the big city. Once I started school, I made friends and life was even better."

"What about the name change? Do you remember being Kayla?"

She shrugged. "Not really. Mom called me sweetie most of the time anyway. Changing my name was part of the adventure."

"She didn't change it much."

"I think she wanted things as close to normal as she could get."

He bit into a ham sandwich thick with mustard. "How'd you know I liked mustard?"

"I saw you put a lot on your hot dog the other day. I pay attention."

The thought of her paying attention to what he did warmed him. He would have liked to have met her under different circumstances. His phone buzzed, and he pulled it from his pocket to glance at the screen. "We're getting a black, female German Shepherd named Shadow late this afternoon. Retired military dog, five years old. She was used to sniff out bombs."

"Shadow. I like that."

"Good, because that's what I want her to be. Your shadow. What's on this mountain other than trees and rocks?"

"Snakes, frogs, bears, deer—"

"People?"

"There's the occasional hunter's cabin and deer stands but not very many. Most of this is government land."

"Any places for people to hide?"

"Like a cave? Sure. There are quite a few of them."

"You'll need to show me someday."

Her brow furrowed. "You think people from New York would resort to hiding in a cave?"

"I'm not willing to rule anything out." He wadded up his trash and shoved it into his pack. "Continue forward or head back?"

She glanced at her phone. "I guess we should head back. We'll need to go into town and purchase supplies for our new family member."

While he hated for the alone time with Karlie to end, he agreed and climbed to his feet.

Once back, he drove to the local superstore where they purchased a large dog bed, a stuffed teddy bear, dog food, dishes, and a container of tennis balls. "You look excited," he said, smiling at Karlie as she filled the shopping cart.

"I've begged for a dog for as long as I can remember." She pushed the cart to the register. "Mom always said they were too much work."

"A puppy would be, but Shadow will be well-trained. We'll be lucky if she chases one of the balls you've bought."

"Oh, she will." Karlie frowned when he insisted on paying for the purchase. "It's my dog, right? I should pay."

"Consider it a gift from your local law enforcement." As they headed across the parking lot, he noticed Mr. and Mrs. Snallings headed in the same direction.

When he turned, they smiled and waved, then continued past them to a black jeep. Nothing about them seemed suspicious. A small town only had so many places to shop, but the hair on the back of his neck prickled. Heath always paid attention to that feeling.

"Did you find a house?" Karlie called after them.

Mrs. Snallings turned. "Yes, we did. A darling little place on the edge of town that is just perfect for me and Ted." Her gaze landed on the dog bed. "Getting a pet?"

Karlie nodded. "We've plenty of room. Have a good day." She headed for the passenger side of Heath's vehicle while he loaded the bags in the back.

He gave the couple a friendly nod, then slid into the driver's seat. Their backgrounds had checked out. Why the suspicion? Because he suspected everyone, that's why. A side effect of his job. Until Bartelloni was behind bars again, Heath wouldn't let his guard down.

They arrived home, right before his friend, Henry Townsend, drove up with Shadow. Henry handed the leash of the beautiful dog to Heath.

"It's her dog." He motioned his head toward Karlie.

He smiled at Karlie and handed her the leash. "She understands German commands as well as English. If you want her to attack without the other person knowing, you say *angriff*. If you want her to simply watch the person, say *uhr*. Here is a folder with all her medical information and a list of German words. You'll be happy with this smart girl. With the handing over of the leash, she knows she belongs to you now."

"Thank you. I love her already." Karlie knelt and held out her hand. "Come here, Shadow."

The dog sniffed her hand, then sat, her wagging tail stirring up dust.

"Everything okay here?" Henry asked, glancing at Heath.

"So far. Shadow here is our newest line of defense. Is it possible to get a Kevlar vest for her?"

Henry snapped his fingers. "Forgot it." He jogged to his truck and retrieved a vest. "I forgot she'll be working. Don't tell the powers that be. The dog is supposed to be retired."

"She's simply being used as protection for Karlie and her mother. But, if trouble comes, I want the dog safe, too." Now, Heath had three females to watch over and found himself outnumbered.

Chapter Six

The Snallings had quickly become regulars at the diner. Karlie had mugs and coffee poured before they could ask for it.

"A lot of places could learn customer service from you," Betty said. "This has to be the friendliest town in the country."

Karlie smiled and left them with menus while she refreshed Heath's coffee. She glanced out the window to where Shadow sat, ears alert, and watched those passing by. A lot of people skirted around the dog even with her leash clipped to a bench. "She is something, isn't she?"

"Absolutely." Again, his gaze rested on her rather than on the object of their conversation.

Her face heated, and she moved to the next customer. The morning sped by, and Karlie collapsed into an empty booth when things slowed enough for her to have lunch. While she ate a chef salad, she tried to come up with ways to keep her and her mother safe while still living life as they had before.

Having Heath close brought comfort, but he couldn't live with them forever. Shadow was a welcome addition, and while she might have been a military dog, she was still only an animal. Maybe an alarm system and cameras to warn them when someone approached the house would be a good idea. Could she get the FBI to pay for it? Her bank account definitely wouldn't cover the expenses, but maybe between her and Mom they could manage.

She glanced up as the bell over the door announced a customer. Two men in suits she didn't recognize entered. Misty Hollow sure was the hot spot to be lately. Since she was on her lunch break, the new girl, Jenny, waited on them.

When she'd left with their orders, one of the men glanced Karlie's way. The hard glint in his eyes sent shivers down her spine. Being one of the few redheads in town might be the very thing to give away her identity. The question now was how did her father find her in the tiny mountain town of Misty Hollow?

Could they have been tracked somehow? Even after twenty years? She shook her head and returned her attention to the food in front of her. She didn't need to invite more worries, especially far-fetched ones. Appetite gone, she carried her plate to the kitchen and watched the strangers from the meal pass-thru window.

"Who are they?" Myrtle asked.

"No idea. Is there some kind of convention in town?"

The other woman shrugged. "Don't know. I did hear that someone bought the abandoned mall on the edge of town and plans on turning it into a hotel. A tourist ploy, I've heard. Maybe they're here about that."

"Hmm." Could something like that have brought the wrong person to their town? The one person who'd alerted Bartelloni about her and her mother? Could it really be that simple? After all, her biological father was looking for a red-haired woman and daughter. The Marshalls weren't the only ones sporting red tresses, but there weren't many. Maybe Bartelloni had spies in other towns, too.

She sighed and headed out to begin the midday rush. When Heath arrived, again leaving Shadow outside since Myrtle refused to allow the dog in the diner, he glanced at the strangers and sat in his usual booth, a shrewd look on his face.

Karlie approached his table and glanced outside. Shadow stared up at the window this time instead of watching the pedestrians. "She seems to sense something."

"Yep." Heath jerked his chin toward the two men. "Newcomers?"

"Yes. Myrtle told me about a new development on the outside of town. Had you heard anything?"

"I'll definitely look into it." He ordered soup and a salad, patting his hard stomach. "Can't eat burgers every day." He grinned.

As if he needed to watch his weight. Refusing to give him the compliment he fished for, she rolled her eyes and continued working. By the end of the day, her feet and back hurt, and she was more than ready for Heath to pick her up and drive her home.

"Want to go with me to check out the old mall after supper?" He asked as they climbed in the car.

"Sure." She turned to nuzzle Shadow. "Did you

miss me, girl?"

"We both did." He winked.

"You see me twice during the day." She clicked her seatbelt into place. "I have to admit that I'm surprised you're asking me to go with you tonight."

"Might be fun wandering around in the dark with you." A dimple flashed in his cheek. He pulled the car away from the curb.

At supper, she brought up the subject of an alarm system. "Any idea how much something like this would cost?"

"I can find out," Heath said. "I know a company that will be discreet and quick."

"I think it's a great idea. We've the money to pay for it." Mom passed a bowl of dinner rolls to Heath. "I didn't exactly leave your father empty-handed."

"Great. You stole not only his daughter but money as well." Karlie shook her head.

"Not exactly. I simply pawned all the jewelry he bought me." She grinned. "Quite expensive jewelry, I might add."

"That's better." Karlie laughed.

After supper, she went to change into clothes more suited to wandering around in the dark with Heath.

~

"I don't like her going out with you this late." Sharon crossed her arms. The dark hid terrible things, and she'd kept Karlie sheltered for a very long time. "She isn't equipped to face danger."

"She'd better learn." Heath narrowed his eyes. "Because it's here. You're welcome to come along."

She shook her head. If someone saw her and Karlie together, one of Bartelloni's men might recognize her or hear Karlie call her "Mom," then they'd know for sure who she was. Sharon had become a prisoner in her own home. "I can't be seen with my daughter."

Resting a hand on her shoulder, Heath smiled. "I'll keep her safe."

"You'll try at least."

His smile faded. "I'll do my best. You have to trust me and Karlie. She has a good head on her shoulders. You've raised her well." He pulled back as Karlie entered the room.

"I hope so," Sharon whispered, pasting a smile on her face to hide her worry.

~

Heath's eyes widened at the sight of Karlie's shapely legs under denim shorts. A black tank top completed her attire, her red hair tied back in a ponytail. Flat canvas shoes covered her feet. She bent to hook a leash onto Shadow's collar, and he swallowed against his suddenly dry throat.

As if she could read the less-than-pure thoughts running through his mind, Sharon smiled and retreated to the sofa. "You two be careful."

"We're only looking around." Karlie straightened. "Do I need anything else?"

"No." But Heath might need a cold shower. Short shorts were a far cry from a shapeless waitress uniform. He rushed to his car, suddenly in a hurry to get the night over with. He parked the vehicle behind the building, out of sight of anyone driving by, and handed Karlie a flashlight. "Keep the dog with you."

"I don't think she'll leave my side. We should let her nose around. You never know what she might find."

True. He turned on his light and turned the

building's corner. "They're going to tear this place down and build a hotel. Nothing too big or fancy, but the town approved it in hopes of bringing in more tourists to the hiking trails and fishing lakes."

"It'll work. There aren't enough places to stay so people drive forty minutes to spend the night somewhere else. Might as well keep the money here in town." She shined her light across the cracked asphalt. "What exactly are we looking for?"

"I doubt we'll find it out here. We'll have to go inside, but we're looking for anything suspicious or that might have a link back to Bartelloni or New York." He pulled a small bolt cover from a hook on his belt and cut the lock on the double doors. The doors squeaked when he pushed them open.

The inside of the mall was pitch black from the plywood covering the doors and windows. Good. It would also keep anyone passing by from seeing their lights. He held the door open for Karlie and Shadow. "Stay together. There are a lot of ways to get hurt in here."

He shined the light upward, revealing missing and hanging ceiling tiles. Some of the glass in the storefronts had been shattered. He lowered his light, shining it along a path of footprints in the dust covering the floor. "Looks like business shoes."

"Which makes sense if men in suits came to check out the property." Karlie shined her light in a circle. "Sad to see something fall into such ruin. I was thinking during lunch...do you think my father could have a tracker on me or my mom? Or is it really as simple as the wrong person coming to our town and seeing how much I look like the woman my mother used to be?"

"Your mother's name used to be Susan Reece. As for the tracker, if he had one, he'd have shown up a long time ago."

"He was in prison."

"Someone else in his organization would have taken you and held onto you until your father's release." He smiled. "I'm sure it's simply someone arriving in town and learning of a young red-haired woman. A case of bad luck."

"For us, not so much my biological father. He must ooze luck."

He chuckled and headed down the wide corridor between the stores. It might have been a hangout for prowling teenagers at one time. A place for women to walk in an air-conditioned place and buy pretty things. Now, the U-shaped building definitely needed to be torn down.

He trained his light on a shorter hallway where the restrooms used to be. Noting a faded staff-only sign, he headed that way and pushed open the door. This place had seen more activity than the main part of the mall.

The floor had been swept clean. A metal desk cleared off. He reached over and pulled a chain. A light overhead glared. "Someone installed electricity."

"Why? There're going to tear the place down."

Heath shook his head. "If we come back in a few days, I bet there'll be computers and filing cabinets. Whatever a mob organization needs to set up a temporary base of operations. Who would expect them to be holed up here instead of a hotel room?"

"A hotel room could be searched," she said. "This is a secret place off limits to the general population and better than a cave in the mountains with no electricity. I bet the bathrooms are working, too. What are you going to do?"

"Let the FBI know. They'll send in someone to keep a watch on things. This is getting too big for me to handle alone." He clicked off the overhead light and held the door open for Karlie.

Back in the corridor, they headed for the main doors.

Shadow huffed low in her throat.

Low voices came from the main entrance.

Heath pulled Karlie into a vacant store and pushed her to a squatting position. He put a finger to his lips.

Placing her hand on Shadow's muzzle, she nodded, her eyes wide before she clicked off her flashlight.

Heath shut his off and waited.

Chapter Seven

"Someone's been here," a man said. "A man, a woman, and a dog."

Karlie's heart dropped to her knees. The target on her back grew two sizes. Misty Hollow was too small to hide in now.

"Stay alert," another man said. "They might still be here."

"Maybe we should leave and come back with reinforcements. I'm not ready to tangle with the sheriff. We'll have to start all over."

Heath tensed beside her. He'd be no match for two men, and she hadn't brought her gun. She vowed this would be the last time she left the house unarmed.

"I'm not comfortable leaving the files here."

"Stop being a baby. Why would they have hung around?"

"Did you see any footprints leaving?" The two men passed by the shop where Karlie and Heath hid. If they shined their light on the floor, they'd see exactly where the footprints ended. Thankfully, they continued on their way.

"Come on." Heath took her hand and peered out of the store. "They're in the office. We'll have to make a run for it. Be as quiet as possible."

In the dark. Without a light. What could possibly go wrong?

Heath motioned for Shadow to lead the way. Karlie kept a firm grip on the dog's collar and let her lead them toward the front of the building. Her foot scraped the floor, and she froze. When no cry of alarm came from behind them, they started again. It wasn't until they stumbled through the dark mall that Karlie realized how far they'd come from the front doors. It seemed like a mile to her, when in actuality it was maybe fifty yards.

Her heart beat so hard she thought Heath could hear. The hand holding Shadow's collar sweated.

Lowered voices from behind alerted her to the fact they were no longer alone in the dark corridor. Her breath came in hitches. Would they hear her breathing?

Heath grabbed her hand and gave a squeeze. His touch reassured her. A gentle tug spurred her to move faster.

"There they are!" The beam of a flashlight broke through the dark.

Shadow wrenched free and turned, taking a stance. Her barks echoed off the walls.

"Come, girl." Karlie switched on her light and sprinted for the doors.

A shot rang out.

Heath stopped and whirled to return fire.

The noise hurt Karlie's ears, but she kept running,

bursting through the front doors and into the moonlit night. "Heath?"

"Right behind you, Darlin'." He grabbed her hand again and they raced for his vehicle.

She barely had her door closed before Heath roared out of the parking lot. She glanced behind them to see the two men in suits making a dash for their car. "They're coming. We can't lead them home."

"I'm smarter than that and, hopefully, a better driver." He pressed the accelerator.

She remained shifted in her seat to keep an eye on their pursuers. "Do you have another gun?"

"In the glove compartment. If you could take out one of their tires, that would be great."

He flashed her a grin, almost seeming to enjoy himself. "Are you having fun?" she asked.

"Nothing better than a good old-fashioned car chase." He ducked as the men behind them shot out the back window.

"How about living to see another day?" Karlie returned fire, aiming at the tire and missing. "That's better than most anything in my opinion."

"We aren't going to die. Your father wants you alive." He yanked the wheel and zipped across the median. "I, on the other hand, am expendable."

Heath wasn't expendable in her eyes. She'd become used to seeing him before she headed to bed at night and then again when she brought him his morning coffee. Her head banged against the window when he whipped the steering wheel to the left, causing her shot to go wild. Shadow whimpered and cowered in the backseat. "Careful or I'll shoot someone I don't intend to shoot. There are other cars on the road." The 911 operator must be very busy with reports of the car chase.

"Sorry. We need to get on a road less traveled." He shot her another grin. "How's this for excitement?"

"Be careful what you wish for, right?" She rested her arm on the back of her seat and took aim. Instead of hitting the tire, she blasted out the front window. "Try not to hit any holes in the road."

"Not much I can do about that." He made a sharp turn onto an off-ramp and weaved through traffic before turning down a two-lane road. "Do you know where we are?"

"The other side of the mountain from home, I think. You need to lose those guys. There's no road home from here without going back through town."

"I'm working on it." Heath sped down a dirt road, spun the car to face the two strangers, and stopped. He shoved his car door open to use as a shield and started shooting.

Karlie did the same. The other car backed up, dust flying, and sped away.

"We didn't take them out of commission, but maybe they'll think twice about messing with us again." Adrenaline burned through her veins. A strange high brought a smile to her face. Excitement indeed.

"Unfortunately, they'll move their base of operations now. We may not be lucky enough to find it again."

Karlie wasn't worried. They'd come for her a second time and a third if that's what it took. "Let's go home. The security people are coming in the morning, aren't they?" She for one was lagging as the adrenaline eased. She climbed back in the car to see Heath staring at her again. How could one look from him send warmth through her? "What?"

He leaned forward, stroking his thumb down her cheek. His hand slowly snaked around her head, pulling her closer. "You are an amazing woman. I'm going to kiss you." The corner of his mouth quirked.

Breathless, eyes wide, she let him pull her ever closer until his lips descended on hers. Strong, soft, gentle, then demanding until her limbs turned to rubber. Here, in the woods, she felt like a teenager necking. With danger around every corner, Heath managed to make her feel safe. Except this was no awkward teenage kiss. This was hot to the very core of her. She wrapped her arms around his neck and returned the passion.

~

The next morning, Heath woke up still feeling the touch of Karlie's lips on his. He'd enjoyed the kiss so much he fully intended to get another as soon as possible. From the moment he'd seen her in the short shorts, he'd wanted to know what it would be like to kiss her. He stretched and sat up, surprised to see Sharon sitting across from him, her gaze locked on him.

"From the mumblings in your sleep, and the smile on your face this morning, I'd say you had quite the night last night. I heard the two of you come home around midnight." Her eyes flashed. "Mind telling me what you were doing out so late with my daughter?"

Was she actually grilling him about a twenty-five-year-old? He rubbed the sleep from his eyes and filled her in on everything except the kiss. His explanation didn't ease the worry from her eyes.

"A shoot-out?"

He nodded. "Karlie held her own. She's really something."

"Yes, she is." She leaned forward. "The last thing she needs right now is a romantic entanglement with a man who'll leave once his job is done."

"Who said I'm leaving? I like Misty Hollow."

Her eyes widened. "You'd leave the FBI to stay as the sheriff of a small town?"

"Maybe." He shrugged. "I'm leaving my options open."

Karlie stepped into the room, dressed and freshly showered, two mugs of coffee in her hands. She glanced from him to her mother, then back to him and handed him his cup. "What's going on?"

"Thanks." He took the cup. "Just filling your mother in on what we found last night." Hopefully, the message in his eyes would keep her from saying more.

She sat on the sofa next to him. "At first, I was scared spitless, but then excitement took over. It was like living in an adventure movie." She smiled around the rim of her cup.

"This is no movie, Karlie. The bullets fired at you were very real." Sharon narrowed her eyes. "This is a life-or-death situation. Don't make light of it."

"I'm not. Heath and I could have died last night. But it still felt unreal after living fifteen years in a town where nothing ever happens."

"I wish it would have stayed that way." Sharon stood. "The security men will be here soon. I'm hitting the shower."

Once she'd gone, Karlie turned to Heath, her voice lowered. "You didn't tell her about...you know?"

He laughed. "Stealing a kiss? I'm not stupid. Your

mother is as protective as a she-bear with her cub." He wiggled his eyebrows. "I do intend to steal another when I can."

Her cheeks darkened. "I'm not a child. She can't dictate my entire life."

"It'll be hard for her to stop after so many years of protecting you."

"I guess so." She sipped her coffee, then set it on the table. "Come on, Shadow. Let's go out before company arrives."

"I'm coming with you." He wasn't taking any chances of her being alone. Shadow provided protection and warning, but the dog couldn't shoot. He grabbed his Glock from the coffee table and followed Karlie outside.

Shadow stood in the yard, ears alert, staring toward the lake. Karlie leaned against the porch railing. "Oh, it's just a squirrel."

Heath followed the dog's gaze, relaxing only when Shadow did. "Good girl. Always alert."

The dog nosed around looking for the perfect spot to do her business. When she'd finished, Heath picked up a tennis ball from the porch and tossed it. Shadow took off after the fuzzy green orb and brought it back. "I'm glad you still like to play, girl."

"She doesn't fall asleep without her teddy bear. Which reminds me I want to look for my stuffed bunny. I'll search the attic after the security guys leave. It'll be good to hold it again, if it's still around."

"Shadow might claim it." He grinned, tossing the ball again.

"Shower's free." Sharon took his place on the porch. "I'll take up guard duty."

Karlie sighed and rolled her eyes. "I don't need twenty-four seven watching here at the cabin."

"Yes, you do." Heath patted her shoulder and headed inside.

By the time he rejoined the women, a truck had pulled into the yard. Shadow stood next to it, her dark eyes fixed on the driver, the hair on her neck raised. Smiles graced the faces of the Marshall women who clearly enjoyed watching Shadow do her stuff.

"Not nice smiling at another's misfortune," he said to the women as he went to greet the man who'd be installing their security system. "Down, girl."

"That dog looks ferocious," the man said, pushing open his door. "Stanley Meyer." He thrust out his hand, keeping an eye on the dog.

"She won't attack unless told to." Heath returned the shake. "Thanks for coming so quickly."

"It pays to have friends in high places." The man grinned and pulled a metal box from the bed of his truck. "I'll have y'all safe and sound in a few hours. Beautiful place you have here. A person wouldn't think you'd need a system so far from town."

"We get lots of bears," Heath said. "Even with a dog, a warning system will be nice." He hated lying, but sometimes it came with the job. He peered into the truck bed. "Are you installing all this alone?"

"No, I've help coming, but it won't be for another hour. He's held up on another job." He hoisted cable over his shoulder. "I'll be fine." Still eyeing Shadow, he headed for the corner of the house.

The man nodded at the women on the porch but didn't pay them much more than a glance. Good. Overdue attention would have made Heath suspicious.

He followed the man. "What's your other guy's name?"

"Harold Downs. Why?"

"Just curious." Heath headed into the house and to his laptop. He wanted to know what the other man looked like. After last night, he wasn't allowing anyone around the Marshall women unless he knew without a doubt that they were who they said they were.

Chapter Eight

Quickly bored watching a man string wires, Karlie headed into the house. In the short hall between the bedrooms, she reached overhead and pulled down the ladder leading to the attic. With nothing else going on, she could search for the bunny. If nothing else, she could browse through childhood memories her mother had stored in the dusty recesses of what was more of a crawl space than an actual attic.

She stayed careful, walking hunched across sheets of plywood laid across the beams and headed to the pile of boxes in a corner. The first one she opened held works of art from her elementary school years. Karlie smiled and flipped through the items. Her mother might have brought her to Misty Hollow to keep her safe, but she'd still acted like a normal mother and kept virtually everything Karlie had made. One day, she'd put the pages in plastic sheets to protect them and show them to her own child.

Closing the box, she set it aside and reached for

another, sneezing as a cloud of dust drifted up and tickled her nose. The second box held clothes but nothing smaller than what Karlie had worn at the age of five and up. Baby clothes would have been left behind as nonessential.

She sat back as a memory assailed her. They'd left with a suitcase and backpack each. Mom had taken only the bare necessities. So much history gone in a run for their lives.

Tears clogged her throat. Don't be such a ninny. Things happen. People lose pieces of themselves all the time. Fires, death, natural disasters. Why should Karlie be any different?

After going through all the boxes and not finding the bunny, she turned to leave, stopping when her gaze fell on an old trunk not much bigger than a bread box shoved in a far corner. The weathered wood blended in with the background of trusses, so she'd almost missed it.

Bending further, she made her way to the trunk and lifted the lid. Envelopes, folders, and the bunny rested inside, shoved together to fit in the small space. These were the things her mother wanted hidden. But why hide Fluffy?

She turned the stuffed animal over in her hands remembering the nights she'd hugged the bunny to her chest, afraid of the way her life had been turned upside down. It bordered on cruelty for her mother to take the bunny so soon after they'd arrived in Misty Hollow.

Stuffing protruded from an area where the threads had been ripped out. She used her finger to poke the white batting back inside and felt something hard. Carefully widening the slit, she pulled out a Jumpdrive.

Blood boiling, she carried the drive and Fluffy down the ladder and into the kitchen where her mother prepared lunch. Karlie set both on the counter. "More secrets?"

Mom planted her hands on the counter and bowed her head. Seconds passed before she spoke. "Why are you nosing around? Some things are best left hidden."

"Fluffy disappeared right after we arrived at this cabin. Obviously to store this drive. What's on it? What's on all the papers in the chest?"

Taking a deep breath, Mom faced her. "The Jumpdrive contains a list of men who work for Bartelloni, men hired to kill, and the names of their targets. The envelopes contain whatever information I could gather on your father, including some things I took from his office."

"You have info on Bartelloni and didn't tell me?" Heath scowled from the doorway. "That's withholding information in an ongoing investigation, Sharon."

"I did what I thought was best at keeping Karlie safe. I thought I could use them as leverage when Bartelloni came for her." She hiked her chin and crossed her arms. "So, arrest me."

His eyes flashed. "That would be a death sentence for you, and you know it." He stepped forward and snatched the Jumpdrive off the counter. "You should have given this to me the moment I moved in here with the two of you."

"How many more secrets?" Karlie blinked back tears, hating the fact they sprang up unwanted whenever she was upset. "I thought we were all in this together."

"The less you knew, the safer you'll be." She

returned to spreading mayo on a slice of bread. "Trouble has come. There's little I can do now." She shrugged. "I suppose it's best you know of the files."

Karlie glanced at Heath. A muscle ticked in his jaw. "I'll go get the trunk. It's small enough for me to carry down myself," she said. "You can weed out what's actually important and burn the rest." Without another glance at her mother, Karlie stormed off.

How could she trust her mother again? She'd just gotten to the point of letting go of the anger from finding out her life had been a lie, and now this. Her mother had lost her mind after all these years. Her reasoning didn't make sense. What would have made sense was turning over the information to Heath immediately.

She pulled down the ladder, climbed it, and headed again to the far corner of the attic. Tires crunched on gravel in front of the house. Grabbing the small trunk, she turned to head back down the ladder only to have it shut on her. What the heck? "Hey." She had no way of opening it from inside.

"Stay there." Heath's voice drifted through the cracks around the door. "I'll let you out when I can. Stay away from the window."

Karlie set the trunk down and moved to the small round window covered by slates. She peered through, barely able to see another truck parked in the yard beside the first. Behind the house, her mother slipped into the woods.

~

She had no more secrets. Nothing to help keep Karlie away from her father. With the drive now in the hands of the FBI, Sharon was defenseless. She leaned against the rough bark of a tree and slid to the ground.

What if she'd stayed in New York? Continued to enjoy the luxuries Anthony bestowed upon her? He'd professed to love her and had doted on his daughter. Maybe Karlie would have been safer there.

No. Sharon still thought it best to take her away from that life. Her father was not a good man, making his riches off the backs and deaths of others. He'd have wanted Karlie to take over someday, would have married her off to a man just like him. Sharon had done the right thing.

Pity party over, she circled back, coming to the trees on the side of the house where the security man worked. With her gun at hand, she watched, wary, untrusting.

With Karlie locked in the attic, Sharon didn't have to worry about her. She narrowed her eyes as the most recent security man clipped something to one of the wires leading into the house.

~

Karlie would be spitting mad when he let her out of the attic, but until Heath confirmed who was in the truck, she'd have to stay out of sight. Sharon had agreed to seek the protection of the thick woods behind the house.

With Shadow by his side, He approached the older model truck. The man who got out of the truck didn't look like the driver's license photo of Harold Downs. Heath kept his hand near his Glock. "You're not the man we expected."

"He couldn't make it." Keeping a wary eye on Shadow, the man exited his truck. "I'm Bill Lowery."

"Stay right there." Heath moved to the foot of the

ladder where Stanley perched at the top. "You know a Bill Lowery?"

"Heard the name but never met the man." He glanced to where the waiting man stood. "Do you want me to let him help? Then I can check things out when he's done."

Heath nodded. "You're as suspicious as I am."

"Figured the story about bears wasn't the whole truth." He climbed down the ladder. "Since the order to install this system came from the FBI, there had to be something big going on."

"You figured right, but I can't tell you any more than that."

"Not a problem. Secrets are part of the job. What set me off was the unusual stillness of your dog. When I arrived, she gave a warning. With this man, she's more like a statue." Stanley introduced himself to Bill, then assigned him the outside work while Stanley moved inside.

"Where do you want the monitors installed?" He asked.

The cabin didn't have a lot of options. "How about the walk-in closet in the master bedroom?"

"Works for me." He carried what he needed to Sharon's room, transferring clothes from one side of the closet to the other. "You can put these back to hide the monitors when I'm done, but I need room to work."

Heath chuckled. "Do what you need to. I'm going out to keep an eye on Bill." First, he looked the man up on the laptop. If he were someone other than who he proclaimed to be, he'd covered his tracks well. The driver's license photo matched the man outside. That didn't mean that the man was clean, though. Most people could be bought.

Stanley stuck his head out of the closet and hollered that he'd phoned the office and Harold had called in sick. "Not normal for old Harold."

Later, Heath would pay a welfare visit to Harold. He needed to reassure himself no harm had come to the man. For now, he'd take Shadow outside and keep an eye on Bill.

Heath sat on a chair on the porch and pretended to read while the man took Stanley's place on the ladder. "Watch him, Shadow," he whispered.

The dog moved to the railing and sat, her dark eyes on Bill. Nothing would get past the German Shepherd's eyes.

Heath glanced upward, glad Karlie had remained quiet, but she'd be watching through the window slats. All he could do was hope she wasn't seen if the man moved the ladder closer to the attic window. He chuckled to himself, thinking of the stories that would circulate around town if Bill were innocent. Tales of a woman locked in a cabin attic in the woods with the town sheriff keeping guard. Shaking off the silly notion, he propped his booted feet on the railing.

Bill climbed down. "Got to move to the other side," the man said. "That dog makes me nervous."

"She won't hurt you." Unless ordered to. Heath peered over the pages of the book he wasn't reading and hoped the man wouldn't recognize it as a romance novel. He'd grabbed the first book he'd seen.

"Looks like she wants to eat me for lunch." He carried the ladder to the other corner of the house and repeated what Stanley had started on the other.

"I'm done inside." Stanley stepped onto the porch.

"Bill, you can move on to the next job. I'll finish up here."

"You sure?" The man glanced down. "We'll finish faster with two."

"Only got the one ladder."

"Okay." Bill climbed down and shook his head. "The Widow Morrison said she's had a Peeping Tom and wants a camera installed in her bedroom and bathroom. I'll head over there."

When the man left, Stanley turned to Heath. "That's the truth. The man must be on the up-and-up. The widow's request came in yesterday."

"Seems strange that you've never met the man, though." Heath set the book aside.

"It does."

Heath went to free Karlie. "Want to take a ride with me?"

"Don't ever do that again," she said, shoving the trunk at him. "I'm dying of thirst and starvation."

He laughed. "We can eat first. I didn't want the new guy to see you. I'm sorry."

Frowning, she made a dash for the kitchen and poured herself a large glass of iced tea, then grabbed a sandwich from the fridge. "I know enough to stay out of sight, but I could have gone to the woods with Mom or stayed in my room."

"There'll be cameras installed in your room."

She rolled her eyes. "Where are we going?"

"To check on the man who should have been the one to help Stanley." He grabbed a sandwich for himself. "The new guy seems on the up-and-up, but Stanley doesn't know him, and the security firm he works for isn't that big."

"You think something happened to the other guy?"

He nodded. "I want to check. And while I trust Stanley, I still don't want to leave you alone with him. Sharon won't be back for a few hours. Went fishing."

"That's what she does when she wants to be gone for a while." Karlie stared at him over her glass. "Next time you lock me up, give me a warning and hand me a bottle of water."

Chapter Nine

"Seems like we're always in your car lately."
Karlie clicked her seatbelt into place, then pushed
Shadow's big face back over the seat. "You're drooling
on me, silly girl."

"We have been around a lot lately." Heath backed
from the drive and headed for town.

"You look worried." She stared at his stern profile.

"Really don't want to find a dead guy."

"But, you said the second man checked out." A
heavy weight settled in her chest.

"On paper, yes."

Karlie drummed her fingers on the armrest, then
blurted out the question niggling at her mind, "Can we
trust my mother? I mean, she's so blinded by the years
of keeping me away from Bartelloni that I don't think
she's making rational decisions right now."

"Very astute of you." He cut her a sharp glance. "I
don't know how much we can trust her, especially after
withholding the Jumpdrive, but I don't think she'd

willingly put you in harm's way."

"You don't think she'll make a dangerous mistake?" Karlie's heart skipped a beat. She'd done a lot of thinking while locked in the attic. Having Heath agree, even partly with her fears, shocked her. She'd thought maybe her feelings were unwarranted.

"Your mother knows how dangerous Bartelloni is. She'll be careful, maybe too careful, as in keeping things hidden that should be brought to light. Sharon is definitely terrified of your father." He reached over and patted her hand. "Stay smart, stay alert, and we'll get out of this alive."

He didn't add to keep an eye on her mother, but she would, most definitely. With the possibility of more secrets, Karlie's heart ached at knowing she couldn't trust her mother—her one constant for twenty years. She blinked back tears and stared out the window, lost in her thoughts until Heath pulled into the driveway of a small house with white siding badly in need of paint.

"Stay close and keep your gun handy." Heath shoved open his door. "Shadow, go to the house."

The dog jumped from the car and, nose down, and approached the wraparound porch. She stopped at the front door and barked.

Heath pressed the doorbell. When no one answered, he turned the doorknob. The door swung open. "This doesn't look good."

No, it didn't. Karlie followed him into the dark house with all the curtains drawn. She glanced around the small living room, taking note of newspapers piled on the coffee table and a half-empty coffee mug next to them. She felt the sides of the cup. Cold.

In a dish on a small table near the door nestled a

set of car keys. "I don't think he went anywhere."

"Maybe he really is sick. Let's check the bedroom."

Hoping they'd find a man sleeping soundly in his bed, Karlie followed Heath down an L-shaped hall past a bathroom in shades of pea soup, past a small bedroom with a twin-sized bed covered with a handmade quilt, and into a larger room with a four-poster pine bed. The bed had been made. "Maybe he's outside?" Or maybe he wasn't home after all. She swallowed past a dry throat.

Heath parted the curtains and glanced out the window. "There's a shed in back. Shadow, lead the way."

She glanced up, barked once, and headed out the door Heath opened. Her pace increased the closer she got to the shed, then she stopped and sent up a frenzy of barking.

"He's in there," Karlie said.

"Mr. Downs?" Heath pushed open the wooden door.

Shadow whined and stepped back.

"Great," Heath muttered. "You might want to stay back, Karlie."

"What if it's a trap?"

"I think it's a dead body. Most dogs don't like the smell of death."

She sniffed. "I don't smell anything."

"I doubt he's been dead long." Heath stepped inside, Karlie right behind him.

Lying on the floor, a screwdriver sticking out of his chest, was a man in his fifties. Blood pooled beneath him.

"Does this mean the other guy killed him?"

"I don't know. But I'll be paying a visit to Bill Lowery." He called the homicide into the office, then looked up Bill Lowery's address. "We'll head there once this scene is processed."

Karlie nodded and rushed from the shed. She didn't blame Shadow for cowering. Death wasn't something she wanted to be around either. With a snap of her fingers, she headed to the small deck at the back of the house with Shadow at her heels and took a seat in a rusty lawn chair reminiscent of the 1950s. She watched Heath pacing around the shed, his gaze on the ground. He'd stop and study something, then move on, until he'd made a complete circle around the small building. A few minutes later, he joined her on the deck.

"Two sets of footprints, one which matches the tread on Mr. Downs's shoes."

"Someone killed him in order to take his place at the cabin. Does that mean the security system is compromised?"

"My friend, Stanley, promised to check things out for anything wrong before leaving. If Lowery added anything to the original schematics, he'll make it right. It'll be safe when we return."

"But it will have given away the location." Her blood chilled.

"Maybe. Think it might be time to move."

"Not happening." She set her jaw. "We stay and face the trouble."

"I was afraid you'd say that."

~

Heath would do some perimeter safety measures of

his own. He knew of some booby traps and early warning systems that would slow down any uninvited guest.

In a small town the size of Misty Hollow, it didn't take long for Deputy Wood to arrive.

"Things sure have picked up since you came to town, Sheriff." He shook his head and hung crime-scene tape around the shed. "Not in a good way, either."

"My apologies, but trouble arrived here twenty years ago." He smiled at Karlie and went to help Wood.

"Yeah? Before you came, all we had to deal with were a couple of meth heads and rowdy teenagers on the weekend." He glanced into the shed and shook his head. "A rotten shame. Downs was a good man. His wife died of cancer a little over a year ago. No kids. He is—was—a deacon at Misty Hollow Community Church."

"We'll find out who killed him." Heath clapped the deputy on the shoulder. "If you can wait here for the crime-scene investigators, I've a suspect to investigate. Know anything about a Bill Lowery?"

"Sure. He's kind of a loser but smart enough. Makes a living by helping wherever he can get a job. You think he did this?"

"He's a person of interest. Is he dangerous?"

Wood's brows rose. "If he killed Downs, he is. Doesn't seem the type, though, but I've heard he'll do almost anything if the price is right."

That's what Heath was afraid of.

"Go on," Wood said. "I've got this."

Heath fetched Karlie and Shadow, then drove a few blocks to a house more run-down than the one they'd just left. If Lowery was making money, he didn't spend it on his house. Rotten boards left a porch looking unsafe. The siding had peeled so much it looked as if the house had leprosy. A board covered the front windowpane. The place looked deserted. Heath called Stanley. "Has Lowery finished the job at the widow's house?"

"Not that he's reported, but you were right about him. The other lady saw Bill doing something suspicious and informed me. I found some bugs in the security system. Nothing too major but enough to make the system not work properly, even shut down randomly at times."

Heath exhaled slowly, casting a look at Karlie. "Could it have transferred the location somewhere?"

"Nah, it wasn't that kind of a bug. I think someone already knows the location if they sent Lowery to mess up the system."

Heath agreed. Unfortunately, he also knew he wouldn't be able to persuade the Marshall women into relocating. Unless they went into hiding, moving wouldn't do any good long-term anyway. "What's the widow's address?"

"Hold on. I'll look in the book." A few seconds later, Heath told Karlie the address and she wrote it on the back of a receipt he'd stashed in the glove compartment. "You finished at the house?"

"Yep. Let me know if you have any trouble, and I'll come back out."

"Thanks." Heath hung up. "Supposedly, Lowery is on a job," he told Karlie. "We'll find out soon enough." Feeling as if he'd be driving around the entire town before the day was through, he drove to the other side and stopped in front of a duplex. The widow Morrison lived in the one on the left and answered the door at Heath's knock.

"Hello, Sheriff. I heard you were good-looking, but you're better than the rumors." A woman in her late forties, wearing a dress one size too small, grinned and winked.

"Thank you, ma'am. Did you have cameras installed today?"

Her smile faded. "I was supposed to, but no one has shown up. Can I file a report with you about a Peeping Tom?"

"I can take your information, but it would help if you went to the station." Heath pulled a small pad from his pocket. "Can you describe the person?"

"Dark, shifty eyes. Wears a camouflage bandana over the lower half of his face." She leaned against the doorframe. "Not quite six feet since all I could see over the windowsill were his eyes. Big feet. He left prints in my flower bed. Wanna see?"

Heath sent a quick text to Stanley alerting him to the fact the widow still needed her cameras installed, then followed her around the building. A black cat hissed at the sight of Shadow and darted under a bush, peering at her with yellow eyes.

In the moist soil of a flower bed were two distinct footprints. Heath snapped a photo with his phone. "I suggest you keep your blinds closed when showering or dressing, ma'am. At least until we catch this guy." Cameras would help with his identity.

With a promise of doing everything he could to help her feel safe, Heath led Karlie and Shadow back to the car. "At least we didn't find another dead body."

"Didn't find the suspect either." Karlie sighed. "It doesn't feel as if we're getting anywhere in catching my father."

"When we return to the house, I'll look over the Jumpdrive and the contents of the chest. Maybe we'll find a clue as to his whereabouts."

When they returned, Sharon was in her closet checking the monitors. "Stanley showed me what to do," she explained. "Karlie needs to know, too. There's an alarm that will go off if anyone breaches the perimeter. A thin wire surrounds the house just inside the treeline. I'll show you both where it is. Be careful not to trigger it. He said the noise is earsplitting. If whoever triggers the alarm continues toward the house, a smaller, silent alarm goes off and locks all the doors and windows. If—" she speared them with a glance. "—the alarm is set. Otherwise, nothing more than the screeching will happen. Not all the cameras are up and running yet, but your man said they would be within seventy-two hours. Only the one in the back-porch light is working right now."

"Then we'll make sure to set the alarm every time we go in and out of the house." It would be a pain, but would hopefully keep them alive. "I'm going to set some traps tomorrow. We've had a murder, and the suspect has disappeared."

Chapter Ten

"I know you were up late into the night," Karlie said the next morning. "What did you find out?"

Heath glanced up from his coffee. "We've got quite an impressive list of men who work for, and with, Bartelloni. I've sent the list to FBI headquarters. If we can get as many of them as quickly as possible, it lessens the danger to us." His sharp gaze settled on her mother. "In one of the envelopes were detailed financial records to an offshore account. I checked and it's been emptied."

Her mom's eyes narrowed. "Too bad I couldn't have gotten to it before Bartelloni did, but I didn't know the password. We could have gone to Europe and maybe lived undiscovered and safe for the rest of our lives."

Dear old Dad must have really done a number on my mom. Karlie shook her head. "If you would have taken more than what you did, someone would have surely come before now."

"I'm deadly serious about you not keeping anything more from me, Sharon." Heath reached for his coffee. "I'll lock you up in a safehouse if I find out you're still withholding."

"I'm not." She clasped her hands on the table. "I'm fully willing to relinquish the reins and trust you to keep Karlie safe."

"He'll keep you safe, too, Mom." Karlie frowned.

"I want his focus on you." Worry lines creased her forehead. "I'm tired and don't want to fight anymore. We've had a good life here, but now everything I worked for is going to be lost."

"It won't be lost. Don't give up the fight yet." Karlie gave her a quick hug. "I'll see you after work. Keep the alarm set. I'm leaving Shadow here with you. Keep her by you at all times." She glanced at Heath who nodded.

At the diner, Heath settled into his usual booth. While he pretended to study the menu, Karlie knew two things: He watched everyone who entered the diner and he'd order whatever the day's breakfast special was. The way he narrowed his eyes at everyone, she doubted any bad guys would dare come in while he was there. Several of the customers flinched at his stare as it was.

"You need to be less conspicuous," she said, pouring his coffee. The man did like his coffee. "Myrtle said you're going to scare away the customers."

He handed her the menu. "Guess I'm a little on edge now that the Jumpdrive is out of hiding. If there's a leak in the department—"

"My father has to know Mom took the drive."

"I'm sure he does." Heath mixed creamer into his cup. "It makes me nervous that it's taking him so long to make a move himself. All he's done is send out spies."

"It's better for him if his men are caught and not him. Are you going to search for Lowery today?"

He nodded. "I'm going to do my best to find out where he spends time when he isn't working and ask some questions. If he did kill Downs, it's outside of his normal type of job."

"What if he was threatened?"

Heath's head jerked up. "It wouldn't be outside of what the mob would do to convince an ordinary citizen to do their dirty work. I need to find out whether he has any family. Good thinking, Karlie."

She smiled and took his order to the kitchen, feeling proud of herself. There was more of her mother in her than she'd thought. Her mother always seemed to find the threat, no matter how small. Karlie grabbed two plates from the serving counter and turned to deliver them when her gaze fell on a backpack in the corner, shoved behind the trashcan. "Is that yours, Myrtle?"

"Never saw it before in my life. It doesn't belong to Jenny either."

Karlie set the plates on the correct table and hurried to catch Heath as he headed out the door. "Wait. There's something I want you to see."

"All right."

She led him behind the counter. "We don't know who that belongs to."

Heath paled. "Get everyone out of the diner. Now." He banged on the counter. "Evacuate! Everyone out. Karlie, go with Myrtle out the back door."

"Do you think it's a bomb?"

"Considering there's a wire coming out of it, yeah. Out now." Pain etched his features and fear shadowed his eyes. "As soon as this place is cleared, I'll be right behind you."

"No." She clutched his arm. "Come now."

He shook her off and shoved her toward the kitchen. "Go."

Customers shoved against each other on their way out the front doors. Myrtle called to her from the back door. Karlie locked eyes with Heath and backed away. "Don't die," she said under her breath.

His lips twitched. "I don't plan on it. Go, sweetheart."

She sprinted for the back door as the last customer bolted out the front. Pounding footsteps behind her told her Heath had kept his promise. As she reached the door, the place exploded. The concussion lifted her off her feet.

Heath wrapped his arms around her and rolled under the dumpster as bricks rained down on them. He held her tight enough to almost suffocate her before the debris stopped falling. "Are you hurt?" His voice sounded as if it came from inside a tin can. He ran his hands down her arms, then cupped her face.

"I'm fine. Where's Myrtle?" She crawled from under the dumpster despite Heath's attempts to keep her with him, her ears ringing. "I don't see her."

"There." He raced to where two cars were parked next to the building.

Myrtle had made it halfway under a car before a beam from the building's roof pinned her legs. Karlie dropped to her knees, ignoring her own cuts and stings.

"Myrtle?"

"I'm here. Just get that board off me. Think my leg is broken. Hurts like the dickens."

Heath heaved the board out of the way. A bone protruded from her shin. "Call an ambulance. I need to see if anyone else needs my help." He cupped her face in his hands. "Stay safe. This would be a good time for them to come for you, but I have to see if I can help."

She leaned into his touch. "I understand. I've got my gun. No one is taking me anywhere unless it's with you."

~

It took every ounce of strength he had for Heath to leave the woman he'd sworn to protect. But as the sheriff of Misty Hollow, even if only for what might be a short time, he had other responsibilities.

Why risk killing Karlie by blowing up the diner? Had Bartelloni given up on getting her back alive? It didn't make sense.

A middle-aged man almost made it out, but was now entombed in the bricks of the front wall, his eyes unseeing. A diner drinking coffee one minute. The next minute dead. All for what?

Luckily, the other diners made it to the other side of the street unscathed, except for an older woman who'd suffered a cut on her head in the stampede. . It could have been a lot worse if Karlie hadn't noticed the backpack.

Sirens wailed in the distance. Heath offered what first aid he could before mingling among the crowd. He approached the man and woman who had been seated at the counter.

"Did either of you see anyone leave a navy-blue backpack?"

The man shook his head. "No one, and we were the first customers in the door this morning. We eat at the counter because the coffee is free if you sit there."

Heath rubbed his chin. The pack had to have been left the night before. Cleaning crew? He'd have to ask Myrtle who had access after the diner closed. He hadn't been able to tell if there was a timer. He scanned the crowd for someone who looked as if they didn't belong. He couldn't rule out the bomb being detonated remotely. Which, if Bartelloni wanted Karlie alive, meant someone had been close enough to see her leave the building and knew she'd likely survive.

Bill Lowery hovered in the doorway of the corner drugstore, which now sported shattered windows from the blast. Catching sight of Heath, he darted around the corner.

Heath pulled his gun and gave chase. If he'd had doubts about the man's involvement before now, he didn't any longer. "Halt."

The man ducked into a women's boutique. Heath entered, shoving aside racks of clothes Lowery exited through the back. Women shrieked from behind the counter where they'd taken shelter when the bomb blew.

Heath skidded to a halt behind the building, realizing how far he'd come from the diner. He'd done more than leave Karlie alone; he'd allowed himself to be led away. Switching direction, he rushed back to the diner, relieved to see her next to the ambulance into which paramedics were loading Myrtle.

"Are you all right?"

She nodded. "The crowd got a little too close for a moment, but your deputies pushed them back. There's someone here. I can feel their eyes on me."

Heath instinctively stepped between her and the crowd. "I saw Bill Lowery. Think he was a decoy to lure me away. It worked." He balled his hands into fists. "How could I have been so stupid?"

"You were doing your job." She placed a calming hand on his arm. "Look at it this way. I won't be going to work for a while so I'll be a prisoner at home where you can keep an eye on me twenty-four/seven—"

"Until they blow up the cabin, too." He doubted that was true, but they *would* come for Karlie and wouldn't care what happened to him or Sharon. "I think we need help."

She arched a brow. "Another FBI agent?"

"Perhaps. I'll contact headquarters and see what they advise."

"Can we go home?" She swiped at a cut on her cheek. "The paramedics said to clean my minor cuts and abrasions. They sting, but otherwise I'm fine. Feel like I'm target practice out here."

"Let me talk to Baines and Wood, then we'll go. Stay here. Even better, get in the ambulance out of sight." He marched over to his deputies. "I've got to get Miss Marshall out of here. Can you handle this? I'll be in tomorrow, bright and early, to take care of the paperwork."

"The mob will risk anyone's life to get to her, won't they?" Baines looked surprised. "I mean, I've heard how ruthless they are, but a lot of people could have died today. I thought working in a small town would be safer than a big city."

"Didn't we all?" Except Heath. He'd known of the possible danger. Karlie would be beating herself up over the day's events once the shock wore off. He needed something to keep her busy, but there wasn't a lot to do at the cabin other than fish, hike, or skip stones.

He retrieved Karlie from the ambulance and kept a wary eye on the crowd while they headed to his car. He knocked a brick from the roof where it had shattered the rolling lights, glad they'd left Shadow with Sharon. The dog would have certainly been killed tied up to an outside bench.

"We're going to have to use me as bait," Karlie said in the car.

"I've told you before that we will not." He shot her a harsh look. "Using you as bait will not put Bartelloni back behind bars."

"But it will get you closer to him. If I'm inside, I can find a way to get him out in the open."

"This subject is closed." He turned the key in the ignition and turned on the siren so pedestrians would move out of his way. "Besides, he's too smart to fall for it, especially if he becomes aware we turned in the Jumpdrive. You anger him enough, and he won't hesitate to kill you, daughter or not."

His cell phone buzzed, and he fished it from his pocket. Seeing it was a text from Sharon, he handed it to Karlie. "Would you mind checking to see what she wants?"

Karlie glanced at the screen and gasped. "The perimeter alarm went off at the cabin."

Chapter Eleven

"Mom?" Karlie sprinted for the house, out of the car before Heath put it in park.

The alarm wasn't blaring. Was that a good sign?

Her mother stood in the kitchen staring out the back door. "The breach came from the left-hand corner of the yard. I turned off the alarm to shut it up. We can reset it now that you're home."

"Could it have been an animal?" Karlie glanced at Heath.

"Would have to be something bigger than a rabbit." He took her mother's place at the window. "Have you seen anything at all?"

"Nothing. Not even a bird. That means something is still out there."

"Let's go find them." Karlie glanced from her to Heath. "Bring them in and ask questions."

"Your mother and I would be picked off before we reached the trees." Heath pulled the shade, opening it just enough to see out. "We'll have to wait for nightfall."

"Ever heard of night-vision goggles?" She plopped into a chair.

"What happened to the two of you?" Sharon seemed to notice their dusty clothes for the first time.

"Someone blew up the diner, then attempted to lure Heath away."

Sharon whipped around to face him, high spots of color on her cheeks and sparks in her eyes. "You left Karlie's side?"

"I do have a job to do in this town in addition to protecting the two of you. If I don't do my job as sheriff, too many people will ask questions. My cover will be blown, leaving the two of you more vulnerable. Do you have a first aid kit? Karlie's cuts need tending to."

"I'll take care of my daughter, since you seem unable to do so." She shoved past him and headed down the hall.

"Don't take it personally." Karlie smiled past the tension. "You should have seen her the time I walked away from her in a store and she couldn't find me for fifteen minutes. Livid and terrified all at the same time."

"You're my daughter." Mom appeared and set a plastic container on the table, then filled a bowl with warm water. "None of this would mean a thing if something happened to you."

"Well, don't blame Heath. I had my gun, and he was helping the wounded. Be happy that I'm locked up here with you until Myrtle reopens."

"How can you presume I'd be happy about the diner being blown up and people injured?" Her mother stiffened, the hand pouring disinfectant into the bowl paused. "Someone could have been killed."

"Someone was. A wall fell on him. They waited until I was out of the diner to set off the bomb. My father apparently doesn't want me dead."

"Who died?"

"Leroy Horace." Tears sprang to her eyes. "He came in every morning for two cups of coffee."

"Why didn't someone shoot you while Heath was chasing after the man who set off the bomb?" She glanced at Heath.

"Too many people around would be my guess. I don't think I was supposed to make it out alive. They didn't figure that the people could evacuate before the bomb went off. Luckily, no one thought twice about heading outside." He parted the blinds a little more. "I'm calling for backup. I need someone else here."

"How will you know if they can be trusted?" Mom dabbed at a cut on Karlie's face.

"I'll request someone I've worked with before. Stay away from the windows and keep an eye on Shadow. She'll alert you if anyone crosses the perimeter."

"What about your booby traps?" Karlie asked.

"I'll have to set them after dark." He strode out of sight.

Mom took care of Karlie's cuts without a word. Her shoulders sagged as she dumped the bowl in the sink. "Maybe I am glad you won't be working for a while." She gripped the edge of the sink. "I'm sorry how it happened, but you're right. Heath has a job and could be called away at any time. That leaves me to keep you safe as I have all these years."

Karlie stood and put a hand on her mother's shoulder. "I'm not a little girl anymore. I can do my part in staying safe. We're a team now. It'll be easier on all three of us if you realize that."

"I'm trying." Tears filled her eyes. "Twenty years of habits are hard to break."

"I know." Karlie wrapped her arms around her in a hug. "Trust Heath. He shielded me with his body today. He didn't want to leave me to go help the other people. I could tell it tore at him. Heath would take a bullet for either one of us. I know that in my heart. I like him, Mom, more than like actually."

A soft smile graced her face. "I can see that. Maybe that scares me more than facing your father. Someday, when this is all over, you'll find a man to marry and have a family of your own. I'll be fine all alone."

"You'll never be alone. You'll be the best grandmother in the world, if not a little over-protective." Karlie chuckled. "Maybe you'll even relax a little in your old age."

Her mother laughed. "I doubt it. Old habits, remember?"

Heath hovered in the doorway. "There's no one to spare. All agents are busy rounding up the names from the Jumpdrive."

Had he heard her tell her mother how she felt about him? Her face heated. "Then it's up to us," she said, taking her mother's hands. "We're all we need."

~

Clouds played hide-and-seek with the moon, making working at setting traps difficult. Heath had reluctantly agreed to let Karlie and Sharon stand guard with Shadow, everyone wearing a Kevlar vest.

Sharon had located some bear traps in the crawl space under the cabin's front porch. Heath set them at irregular intervals and covered them with dead leaves and other foliage. Now, he worked at stringing fishline covered with hundreds of sharpened fishhooks in as many open spaces as he could. He also wanted to dig some pits and set tiny bombs where the bear traps weren't. Using a shotgun shell as a land mine, buried in the dirt, could effectively stop the person who stepped on one.

Karlie had the job of spraying a spot of yellow on trees that would provide a safe path for the three of them to enter the woods if they needed to. "Shadow will have to be on a leash if we leave the yard."

Heath nodded, intent on his work. A twig snapped to his left. He turned and strained to see through the dark. If they were being watched, the traps would be useless. The head lamp attached to his forehead illuminated the eyes of a deer. Best stay away, little lady, or you'll be used to fill the freezer.

"Where did you learn how to do this?" Karlie sprayed a tree next to him.

"Books." He flashed a grin. "And the internet. You can learn almost anything from those two sources."

"Lord help anyone who gets tangled in that web." She nodded at the fishline. "You're covering a lot of territory with that."

"It won't kill anyone," he said, "but it will make them think twice about proceeding."

"Or make them very angry. If they come near the cabin, I'm not going to worry about whether or not they live." Sharon moved next to her daughter. "I plan on shooting to kill."

"At least let us catch one bad guy so we can interrogate." The woman was bloodthirsty.

"Fine. I'll shoot the first one in the leg."

Karlie laughed at the conversation between the other two and glanced toward the cabin where an unhappy Shadow had been tied to the back deck. Poor girl. She wasn't used to being left alone. "What about the front yard?"

"No one can get close to us that way. Not without being seen. I'll set traps everywhere a body can sneak up on us, but I don't want to endanger us or a friendly visitor." Heath cut another length of line. "If you get tired, go back. This will take all night."

"With no job to go to, I can sleep in."

There'd be a lot of lying around with nothing much to do. Heath would only leave if something came up the other two deputies couldn't handle. Wood would cover the day shift and Baines the night. Other than that, Heath would be as bored as the two women. Maybe he'd take up fishing. Buy a boat and take Karlie out on the water.

His mind drifted to Karlie while he continued to spin his web of hooks. He might catch something far bigger than he intended. If a bear came through, it would tear everything down and become enraged. No help for it. But it was the two-legged predators that worried him the most. A loud noise and pepper spray wouldn't stop the men who worked for Bartelloni.

As the early morning hours passed, Heath decided to call a halt. The women looked dead on their feet, and his shoulders ached from the work. Digging pits would have to wait until the next dark. During the day, he could sit inside and build coverings that would collapse under a man's weight.

"Come on, ladies. That's enough for now." He led them home, turned off the alarm, then turned it back on once everyone was inside. Already the act of on and off grew old. Still, they couldn't be careless. One lapse of judgment could be a fatal mistake.

The women shuffled off to bed. Heath toed off his shoes and fell, clothed, onto the sofa, not bothering to fetch his blankets. Sleep overtook him almost immediately.

Shadow's frenzied barking woke him at dawn right before the alarm screeched. The dog faced the front door, hackles raised.

Heath grabbed his weapon and peered through a slit in the curtains. A white Ford truck had turned around in the drive and now sped down the road leaving a cloud of dust in its wake. Simply someone losing their way or an intruder scared off by the alarm?

Was Bartelloni's men testing the perimeter? If it had been them setting off the back alarm yesterday, were they trying the front today?

As Karlie and Sharon exited their rooms, Heath turned and entered Sharon's room. "If those cameras aren't up and working by now, I'll be calling Stanley."

He sat on a stool and turned on the monitors. Bingo. Cameras mounted in strategic places showed every corner of the front and back yards and every room in the house except the bathroom. He watched as the Ford truck raced down the dirt road toward the house, skidded to a halt, and abruptly turned into the drive.

A young couple sat in the front seat, grins on their

faces. Simply some teenagers out for a joy ride.

He turned to the Marshall women, the same grin on his face. "We're up and running now."

Chapter Twelve

After being awakened by the security alarm, Karlie had a hard time going back to sleep. When she finally did, she slept until almost noon. She climbed out of bed and stretched, her mind trying to come up with something to do to fill the rest of the day. Not much of a television watcher, she could read a book but not for hours and hours. She shuffled past the living room where Heath weaved thin branches together. "Trap doors?"

He nodded. "I've already got my coffee. Pot's still hot." He glanced up and smiled. "You're beautiful when you first get out of bed with your rosy cheeks and mussed-up hair."

Her hand went to smooth her hair, and she entered the kitchen, desperately wanting him to kiss her again. She thought about being the one to make the move until she saw her mother seated at the kitchen table. With a sigh, she poured a cup of coffee and stared out the window toward the woods. "I wish this was all over with. Staying cooped up in this cabin will accomplish nothing but drive me crazy. My father has to know we're waiting for him. We need to draw him out."

"Heath will come up with a plan. Be patient."

"Not one of my virtues." She took a sip of her coffee and rejoined Heath in the living room. "Mom said you're working on a plan."

"I'm mulling one around in my head."

"Mind sharing?" She arched a brow.

"I don't have it all worked out yet, but I'm trying to devise a way to wreak enough havoc with his minions so Bartelloni is drawn out of hiding to come for you himself."

"Sounds good. What's the first step?"

"Finding the new hiding place for the men we encountered at the mall. Want to take a ride later?"

"Absolutely." She smiled around the rim of her cup, pleased they had something to do until dark. "There are several vacant buildings and abandoned barns in the area. They'd make good hiding places. If they don't pan out, I'll show you the caves tomorrow."

He nodded and held up a five-by-five-foot "door" covered with leaves. "That ought to cave even if someone your size steps on it. I need to make a few more, but we should go while we have enough hours to search well." He propped it against the wall.

Her mother declined accompanying them, saying someone had to stay and watch over the monitors. She sat in the closet like a miser guarding her gold. "Don't worry about me. The alarm will work. If the doors and windows get locked because of a breach, I'll text you to stay away."

"Like that will happen," Karlie muttered, leaving

her alone. Heath would have them back to fight alongside her mother as fast as he could. With Shadow by her side, Karlie joined Heath outside next to his vehicle. Every line of his body showed tension as he scanned the yard. He'd parked his car as close to the house as possible.

"The most danger is from the house to the yard." He held her door open for her.

"Then don't wait in the open anymore." She let Shadow in the back seat, then climbed in the front. "Come out when I do or wait in the car."

"I came out early to move the car up to the porch." He turned the key in the ignition and drove toward town.

"There's a warehouse on the east end. It's large and run-down. The area is overgrown with trees and bushes. Would make a mighty good hiding place."

"I want to stop at the station first to check in." Ten minutes later, Heath left Karlie waiting in his office while he went to talk to Baines. When he returned, Baines escorted them back to the car.

"Everything is quiet. Which seems strange with the mob in town," Baines said. "We're being vigilant and were told we'd have backup as soon as some officers are available. Maybe this will be over before then."

"We can always hope." Heath nodded before backing from the parking spot and heading for the east end of town.

"It has to end eventually." Hopefully with no more deaths. Annie's death and the poor man killed by the falling wall were already too many. Karlie worried more for her mother and Heath than for herself. Both would step between her and danger when it came, despite her telling them she could do her part in bringing down her father. She glanced at Heath's strong profile. If things got too bad, she'd have to take matters into her own hands. "Turn right at the stop sign."

A few minutes later, they stopped in front of a block building. Karlie peered through the windshield. "It doesn't look as if anyone is here. The door is padlocked."

"We still have to take a look. Keep the dog and your gun handy." Heath shoved open his door and paused. When nothing happened, he jumped out and released Shadow from the back.

Karlie stayed close by his side as they approached the building. She cupped her hands around her eyes and peered through a grimy window. "I can't see anything."

"Maybe we can enter through the back." Heath headed around the corner. "There's a broken window. Here's to law enforcement and unlawful entry." He picked up a tree limb as thick as his wrist and broke out the rest of the glass. "I'll go in first. If it's safe, help the dog through, then follow her."

When Heath gave the all-clear signal, Karlie didn't have to do anything but stand back as Shadow leaped through the open window. It wasn't as easy for her short stature. She gripped the windowsill and flung a leg over.

Heath put his hands on her waist and lifted her through, letting her slide down the length of him before releasing her. "I think we're alone." His lips twitched.

"Oh?" She smiled and glanced around the dark, dingy building. "Not a very romantic place, though, is it?"

"I don't care." Using his forefinger, he turned her

face back to his. "It's rare that your mother's eagle eyes aren't on us. I have to admit I'm a little afraid of her."

"Big baby. What are you waiting for?" She raised up on her tiptoes and closed her eyes.

~

Heath held her as close as humanly possible and claimed her lips, relishing in the softness of them. Danger still loomed outside, hidden, waiting to pounce, but even that could wait for a few minutes. The feel of Karlie's lips against his helped erase the tension in his shoulders. The soft moan in her throat increased the passion of his kiss until they were both breathless. His heart raced as if he'd sprinted a mile. Pulling back slightly, he rained kisses down her cheek and neck, then back to her mouth.

Shadow huffed as if to say, 'enough already,' then turned to explore.

Karlie laughed. "We've been brought back to the task at hand."

"I'll come up with more reasons to get you alone, no doubt about that. I kinda like kissing you." He landed one on her cheek, then turned to follow the dog.

No footprints other than Shadow's disturbed the dust on the floor. The cavernous room held no furniture or boxes. No one had been there for a long time. He strode down a short hallway, glancing in rooms that might have been offices at one time. "There's nothing here. Where's the next place on your list?"

"Just a few miles away. Since the economy is just starting to grow in Misty Hollow, there are way too many vacant buildings. Hopefully, the new hotel—if it's actually going to happen—will help."

He helped her back out the window and followed,

Shadow sailing through with little effort. Ten minutes later, they parked outside an office complex and discovered it empty except for sleeping bags and drug paraphernalia. Heath called it into the station.

The next stop was an out-of-business bank. This looked promising. The boarded-up windows would give privacy to anyone inside and the chain bolting the two front doors together had been cut. Since there were no cars in sight, Heath felt it safe to proceed.

He opened one of the doors wide enough for them to squeeze through. The boards on the window prevented sunlight from penetrating, and he pulled a small flashlight from his pocket, shining it on two sets of footprints leading to the back of the building. He glanced at Karlie and grinned.

They followed the prints to a room with a computer. A cursor blinked on the screen showing electricity had been restored to the building. He'd have to find out by whom. On one wall were three photos of red-haired women. Karlie was one of them.

"Bingo. We need protective custody on those two."

Heath nodded. "They aren't sure which one is you, which might work in our favor. They couldn't have gotten a good enough look at you that night at the mall." He used his phone to take photos of the other two women and sent them to Baines to put through facial recognition immediately. Karlie was right. These women needed protecting, unaware their lives were in immediate danger. He grabbed the laptop from the desk. "We need to return to the office." He darted from the building, barely pausing long enough to close the door.

Shadow raced ahead of them, then stopped, all four

feet planted on the asphalt. When Heath went to move around her, she blocked his way, growling, then bared her teeth. It took a second for it to register in his mind that she was a bomb dog.

"Get back, Karlie. Come, Shadow." He backed slowly away, then grabbed Karlie's hand and ran to the back of the building, the dog on his heels.

The shock of the explosion rocked the bank, but the brick walls held. Whoever put the bomb on his car had to have been close enough to know when to press the trigger.

"Good girl." Karlie sagged against the wall, pulling the dog into a hug. "You saved our lives."

Heath had been careless. He should have known a car bomb was a possibility and parked out of sight. Unless…they'd been followed. It would have to have been from the station.

He glanced at Karlie. She'd been right behind him, shielded by his body and might have survived the blast. He and Shadow would have been dead. Whoever pressed the trigger would also know they got away. Who did they think Karlie was? A different possibility than Bartelloni's daughter? A cop? They weren't taking any chances at killing her until they knew for sure?

"We have to get out of here." He searched for an avenue of escape.

To their right was a large drainage ditch leading to a culvert they could crawl through if they hunched over. If they could make it there without being seen, they might have a chance of escaping with their lives. "Follow me and stay low."

Bending over, he pulled her after him, jumping into the ditch and lying flat. When no shots came, he sprang up and made a dash for the culvert. Inside its concrete protection, he stopped and listened again before continuing under the road and emerging behind another building. They sloshed through murky water and decaying leaves until reaching a place still in business. Then they slipped through the back door.

Teenage workers in the fast food restaurant turned to stare at the dusty strangers with a dog. Ignoring them, Heath led Karlie and Shadow through the kitchen and into the eating area. There, he peered out the window for signs of pursuit.

"You need to start dressing like a police officer," he told Karlie. "It might make them more unsure about your true identity." He hated the fact it would also make her more expendable.

"That's a very good idea." She plopped into a booth while Heath called for Baines to come pick them up.

After a few minutes, Heath ushered her up. "Our ride is here. We're going out the back." They hurried past the surprised teens again to where Baines waited in his squad car.

"Wood was right," the rookie said. "Things sure are interesting with you around."

~

Sharon glanced from the television as Heath and Karlie entered the house. The dog headed straight for her food dish. "Why are you dressed as a cop?"

Heath explained about the car bomb. "Once again my daughter was almost killed under your protection," she forced through clenched teeth. "It's better she remain here with me from now on."

"No." Karlie hiked her chin. "Death from being

locked up would be worse than death by bullet." She glanced at Heath. "Let me change and we'll start digging those pits." With a sharp glance at Sharon, she headed down the hall.

"Maybe we need someone else watching her. Send you back to where you came from." Sharon wanted to punch the man.

His face darkened. "She's in as much danger here as out there with me." He raked his hands through his hair. "Your dislike of me is irrelevant. Why can't you see that I would die for your daughter?" Pain etched his face.

"It might come to that."

Chapter Thirteen

It wasn't that Sharon disliked Heath, Sharon realized the next morning. It was more the fact her daughter was being pulled away from her. A natural event, considering her age, but why did it have to happen under dire circumstances? She wasn't ready to let her go. Not now.

The possibility that Karlie's pulling away had to do more with her mother's secrets rather than a handsome FBI agent followed Sharon to the kitchen. She put on a pot of coffee and set to work making pancakes. Since it was closer to lunchtime than breakfast, she thought the others might want something more substantial than eggs.

A late night of keeping watch while Heath dug pits left Sharon with gritty eyes and a sullen attitude. Her daughter wasn't the only one who dreaded a lockdown situation. The isolation gnawed at Sharon. She pasted on a smile as Karlie entered the kitchen. "Good morning. Any plans for today?"

"Heath and I are going up the mountain to look for signs of people living in caves. It's a waste of time, but we've exhausted possibilities in town." She leaned against the counter and stared at the coffeepot. "There's nowhere else to look."

"Maybe Bartelloni's men are staying in another town?"

"I can't imagine them being a forty-five-minute drive from here. No, they'll stay close, waiting for a chance to grab Kayla Reece." She gave an audible sigh as the coffee finished and poured two mugs. "What about you?"

"Staying here." Again. She waited for her daughter to invite her along. When no invitation came, she flipped a pancake. "I'll make sandwiches when I'm finished here."

"Is something wrong?" Karlie's brow furrowed.

"Just tired." Keeping her smile in place, she pulled plates from the cupboard.

Karlie tilted her head as if to study her mother, then turned on her heel and carried the coffee cups out of the room.

Sharon's smile immediately faded. Another day alone. Might as well get used to it. There was someone new in her daughter's life now.

~

"Mom seems out of sorts this morning." Karlie handed Heath his coffee, pulling him away from his laptop.

"We had an argument last night about her lack of cooperation with me. Thanks." He sniffed his cup. "I've been up for a while checking online news and information from headquarters. They've managed to nab a few names off the list from the drive. All we have to do is wait until enough of them are behind bars to draw your father into the open."

It wouldn't happen soon enough for Karlie. "Why don't we go to New York and help?"

He stared at her over the rim of his cup. "Just because you'll be wearing a uniform occasionally does make you law enforcement."

"I know that, but Bartelloni doesn't. He'll think I'm another pain-in-the-rear cop getting in his way and hopefully confront us. Any word on the other two women whose photos were in the bank?"

"They've been alerted and put in hiding until this is over."

Good. Less for Karlie to worry about. She couldn't handle another woman dying because of her.

"The bad news is…another woman disappeared. A red head from Culverville." His shoulders slumped. "I'd hoped these events were located only in Misty Hollow."

"She'll be killed, too." Karlie flopped onto the sofa, spilling some of her coffee onto her leg. She swiped off the hot liquid and blinked back tears.

Heath pulled her head to his shoulder. "This will all end soon. I promise."

"How many people will die first?" He'd already showered, the scent of soap filling her senses. She closed her eyes and breathed, loving how she fit into him as if she were made to be at his side.

He rested his cheek against her head, pulling back when Mom entered the room.

"Never mind me. I'm resigned to the fact the two of you are growing to care for each other." She sat across from them. "I'd like to go with you after we eat. Another day stuck here is too much, even for a hermit like me. May I?"

"Of course." Heath straightened. "Your help is welcome at any time."

"I also want to apologize for yesterday. You will do everything in your power to keep Karlie safe. I need to work with you, not against you."

"Thank you." Karlie moved to give her mother a hug. "The three of us are a formidable team."

"We're something, at least." She chuckled. "Pancakes are ready."

After breakfast, with Shadow leading the way, they headed into the woods ladened with backpacks, taking care not to set off any traps. Karlie wouldn't trust navigating them on her own, even with spots of yellow strategically placed, but Heath moved sure-footed in front of them.

"I'm happy for you," Mom said quietly. "He's a good man."

Karlie shot her a quick look. "We're aren't looking ahead any further than today. We don't know what the future may hold. Who knows? He may decide to return to New York. I'm not sure if I want to leave Misty Hollow anymore."

Her mother grinned. "For the right man, a woman will do almost anything. Look how long I stayed with your father."

"So, you did love him?"

"Very much at one time. I would've liked things to have turned out differently." A shadow passed over her eyes.

"Where's the first cave?" Heath glanced over his

shoulder. "We're past the traps now. One of you can take the lead."

"I will." Her mother smiled at her again, then moved to the front of the line. Heath stepped behind Karlie. Even on the trail, they kept her safely sandwiched between them. While it made her feel cherished, she didn't want one of them to die in her stead.

~

When they approached the first cave, Heath sent Shadow ahead of them. The dog didn't look concerned, so the three approached. The cave held nothing but bear scat.

"This is too close to the house for my taste," Sharon said. "I thought the bears were farther up the mountain."

"Let's hope they don't come close to the cabin, or most of my traps are for nothing." Heath shook his head. "Lead on."

The second cave was little more than an overhang. No place for anyone to hide.

"The next one is promising." Karlie put a hand on his arm. "It's far enough from the cabin to prevent anyone from being seen. It's where I thought the bears lived. Maybe someone moved in, causing the bear to find a new home."

"Maybe." Or maybe it was all a waste of time. He couldn't see anyone who worked for Bartelloni being willing to rough it this much. His men were used to luxury. Paid well, they lived in fancy houses and drove expensive cars. If the cave didn't pan out, he'd search Culverville. After someone brought him another squad car. In the meantime, he'd have the local police there search all abandoned buildings.

The third cave was a bust the same as the first two. The highlight of the day so far was spending it with Karlie. Even with Sharon joining them, he'd take what he could get. Out here on the mountain, danger wasn't breathing down their necks like it did in town.

Heath sent a text to Baines, requesting a vehicle be brought to the cabin asap. He didn't like being cooped up any more than the women did.

The sirens were blaring when they arrived back home, a squad car in the yard. Heath led Shadow around the car to sniff for bombs while Sharon headed inside to reset the alarm. Heath smiled, imagining Baines leaving as soon as the alarm triggered. The blaring noise would be enough to drive anyone away. It also let anyone close know they had a security system. Bartelloni's men would have to find a way around the alarm, thus heading right into the traps. In theory, at least.

"I've got work to do at the office," he said, glancing at a text from Baines. "An elderly woman's house had been broken into, and she didn't want anyone investigating but the sheriff. Seems she only thinks the top dog can get anything done. Since this doesn't have anything to do with Bartelloni, Karlie, stay here with your mother. I'll leave Shadow with you."

"No way. I'll stay, but you take the dog. She's the only alert you'll have if someone plants another bomb."

He nodded. "Keep the alarm on and don't go outside." Once the women were safely in the house, he verified by his phone that the alarm was set and headed into town.

Mrs. Westly looked to be approaching eighty and

cracked the door open the moment he pulled into her drive. "It's about time."

"Sorry, ma'am. I was working on something else."

"Well, come in." She led him to a small room at the back of the house. "Someone stole my computer."

Heath stared at the empty desk, then over to the broken window. Before he could speak again, another text about a theft came through from Baines. Another computer. His gut told him the two men who kept eluding him were replenishing their means of operation and didn't want to leave a trail of purchases. Where would they hole up? He took Mrs. Westley's information and advised her to have her window fixed as soon as possible. "I don't think they'll be back. They've taken what they wanted."

"Are you sure? I live here alone, you know."

"Yes, ma'am. I strongly doubt they'll bother you again. Maybe you should consider getting a dog." He smiled and stepped onto the porch where Shadow waited. He rubbed her chin, then headed for the car. Thankfully, no bombs.

A few minutes later, he sat across from Baines. "Are there anymore vacant buildings I may not have investigated yet? The men have to be setting up somewhere."

"What if they've found someone to take them in?" Baines raised his eyebrows. "Maybe we should look at newcomers to town."

"I research every new person who shows up." Still, he had nothing else to go on. "Anyone other than Mr. and Mrs. Snallings move in?"

"Nope. At least, not that I've heard. The local realtor would know. "

Heath headed to his office to make the call and confirmed the Snallings couple were the only new arrivals to town. "Looks like we have a call to make," he told Shadow. "I've been meaning to anyway. Just haven't had the time." Since he was already in town, now would be ideal.

Ten minutes later, he stood on the front porch of a small blue-painted house. Mrs. Snallings greeted him with a smile. "What can I do for you?"

"I'm looking for two strangers in town. Men in their middle thirties. Have you seen anyone like that?" He tried to peer around her.

She moved to block his view, stepping out of the house and pulling the door closed behind her. "My husband isn't feeling well and is sleeping. If he has the flu, it wouldn't be good for you to go in."

Not a trace of pretense crossed her face. If she was lying, she was an award-winning actress. Exactly what a man like Bartelloni would want in a minion.

Chapter Fourteen

The force of the bullet in his back dropped him to the ground. "Down, Shadow." Heath rolled under the car and out the other side, trying to catch his breath. The vest he wore had kept the shot from being fatal, but it hurt like the dickens. The question of whether the Snallings worked for Bartelloni had been answered.

He peered around the car's fender to see Mrs. Snallings, if that was really her name, and her husband on the porch with guns. A few seconds later, two men rounded each corner of the house.

Heath got to his knees and reached into the front of the car for his radio. Shadow jumped into the front seat and barked. "Get down, girl." He held the radio to his mouth. "Shots fired at the Snallings' place. I'm pinned down four-to-one. No way I'm getting out of here without help."

"On my way," Baines said. "I'll get Wood on the way. Hang on."

"Come in quiet."

Heath glanced around for a better place to take cover. There weren't a lot of choices. The Snallings kept the area around the house cleared. He'd have to make a fifty-yard dash to the trees. "Come on, Shadow. Run."

He took off, knowing the dog would be right on his heels. Shots rang out. Fire burned across his left arm. Heath ran in a zigzag pattern. Another shot ripped into his right thigh. Great. He'd been shot on both sides of his body. He'd be mincemeat if he didn't make it to the trees.

Limping now, he dove into a thick bush, rolled onto his knees, and returned fire. It was quite possible he wouldn't make it out alive. He felt the phone in his pocket, wanting to contact Karlie, but left the phone where it was. Why worry her? Either he'd survive or not. Contacting her might bring her into the danger. She wouldn't stay at the cabin if she knew he was in danger.

Instead, he kept his gaze on the house where three of the four people had returned to the house. At least that's how many guns he spotted poking out of open windows. The fourth must be trying to sneak up on him. Wouldn't happen with Shadow on the alert, but the man could try.

Heath now trained his attention on the thick woods. The sun barely broke through the branches overhead, keeping the leaves and ground soft. If someone walked carefully, they could do so without being heard.

Shadow's ears twitched.

Heath put a hand on her muzzle to keep her from barking and giving away their location. "Come," he whispered, slipping from his hiding place. Ignoring the fire in his arm and leg, he hobbled to another bush and crouched low. It wasn't until he collapsed back to the ground that he realized he'd left a blood trail even a child could follow. "We're in a sorry state, girl." He patted Shadow's head.

Heath ripped the sleeve off his shirt and tied it around his arm. He used his belt to help slow the blood from flowing out of his leg. The shot to the arm had only grazed him, but the bullet to the leg had gone clear through. He'd bleed to death if Baines didn't arrive fast.

"All you have to do, Sheriff—" Mr. Snallings called out, "—is give us Kayla Reece. Tell us where she is, and we'll let you die in peace. Otherwise, we'll shoot each of your limbs one-by-one before putting a bullet in your head."

Nice try. No way was Heath going to respond and give himself away. Let them think he was already dead. Maybe they'd get careless.

Rapid gunfire rang out along with the crunch of tires on gravel. The cavalry had arrived. Heath closed his eyes and concentrated on not dying.

Shadow barked.

Heath opened his eyes and stared down the barrel of a gun. "Angriff," he forced the command through gritted teeth.

Snarling, Shadow sprang forward, clamping her teeth around the man's forearm, shaking him like an old rag.

The man screamed. His shot went wild, striking Heath at close range in the chest. That was going to hurt for a while. He fell to his side and curled into a ball, listening to the man's shrill screams as Shadow's teeth broke the skin.

Heath aimed his gun and fired, his shot striking the man between the eyes. "Down, girl." He lost consciousness, his last thought about how glad he was that Shadow had been with him. He came to in the ambulance with Shadow at his side and Baines and Wood staring down at him. "Thanks for coming."

"You're a bit worse for wear." Wood grinned. "Next time, call for backup before the shooting starts."

"I didn't know there'd be shooting until I rang the doorbell and Mrs. Snallings wouldn't let me in the house. Did you get them?"

"Yeah, the mister is dead, along with the man in the woods, but the other two are cuffed and in the squad cars." Wood jumped to the ground. "Want me to call your girl?"

"I'd prefer it if you'd show up, then escort her to the hospital. I don't want her on the road alone."

The deputy nodded. "I'll do that and let Baines take care of booking the shooters." He headed for his car.

Baines stood there with a stupid smile on his face. "I gotta admit that I was a little disappointed when I got assigned to Misty Hollow. Then, common sense set in, and I realized no action was better than getting shot at and killed. Now, there's a new sheriff in town, and this small community is seeing the same action I once thought I'd miss."

"Glad to be of service. Take the dog with you. She doesn't belong at the hospital. Make sure Sharon gives her a big treat." He closed his eyes.

~

Karlie turned off the alarm and stepped onto the porch as a squad car pulled in front of the cabin. When

Shadow leaped out, followed by Baines, her heart dropped to her knees. "Where's Heath?"

Her mother joined her and put an arm around her shoulder. "Don't automatically think the worse."

What else would she think when Shadow was being brought back by a different person?

Baines approached. "He's been shot." He held up a hand at Karlie's cry. "He's alive and will be fine, most likely. This dog saved his life."

"That happens a lot." Karlie choked back a sob and wrapped her arms around Shadow's neck.

"The sheriff wants me to bring you to the hospital. Can you go now?"

"Yes. Mom?"

"I'll stay here with Shadow." She smiled. "I think she deserves a nice steak, don't you?"

"Most definitely." Karlie stepped off the porch and into the squad car. Inside, she turned to Baines. "Are you telling the truth about Heath's condition?"

"Yep. Shot grazed his arm and another went clean through his leg. He's lost a lot of blood, might need surgery, but he'll live." He backed onto the road and turned on his sirens.

Once at the hospital, Baines escorted Karlie inside and into the capable hands of a nurse. "Call me when you want me to come take you home." He turned to the nurse. "Put her in the sheriff's room. No waiting room for this lady. She needs to be within sight of the nurse's station at all times."

The nurse stared at him, then Karlie. "I understand. Follow me, Miss."

Nodding, Karlie followed the nurse to a private room. "The doctor will speak with you as soon as the sheriff is out of surgery," she said. "Leave the door open and give us a yell if you need anything. There's a coffee and juice station right outside."

Karlie sat in the only chair in the room and hung her head. She prayed for Heath's safety and for a quick end to her father's life. She pushed to her feet and moved to the window overlooking a small garden. Who could they trust in Misty Hollow? Anyone, even faces she saw every day at the diner, could be bought if the price was right, or so it seemed.

Heath almost died because of her needing protection. If he weren't assigned to her, she'd send him away for his own safety. As it was, she needed to pull back, guard her heart. If they survived, when life returned to normal, she could determine then if a relationship were possible. For now, she needed to back off.

Two hours later, a groggy Heath was wheeled into the room. "I must have died because there's an angel by my bedside."

"Don't joke." Karlie gripped his hand, choking back tears. "You almost died today."

"Almost being the magic word." His eyes squinted at her. "You should ask for some of whatever they gave me. You look tense, and I feel great." A goofy grin covered his face.

She laughed in spite of her fear. "Go to sleep."

"Will you be here when I wake up?"

She nodded, wanting to say no but knowing she couldn't. Not until she knew he truly was on the mend.

As Heath's eyes drifted closed, a doctor entered the room. "Miss Marshall, I presume." He glanced at the chart in his hand. "He listed you as someone we could divulge his medical treatment to. We stitched his arm, repaired his leg, and he'll be out of here tomorrow if things go well. He'll need to take it easy on his leg for a while, but Sheriff Westbrook is a strong man."

"Thank you." Karlie resumed her seat in the chair. Having Heath disabled for a while would allow her to formulate a plan, then execute it without him coming after her. It might take a few days for her to implement what was fermenting in her mind, but then...well, things would be forced to come to a head.

Hopefully, Heath would forgive her for the deception. If she survived.

~

Sharon set a plate on the porch with a rare steak on it in front of Shadow and sat in the rocking chair nearby. Karlie had been gone for hours. No news was good news, right? She shook her head. Sometimes, it simply meant the news hadn't been sent and received.

Nursing her third cup of coffee wasn't helping any. Every nerve seemed high-wired as she lifted the cup to her lips with trembling hands.

It was nearing dark before Deputy Baines brought Karlie home. Sharon didn't want to look too worried but lunged to her feet anyway. Since she chose to sit outside, she'd left the alarm off until Karlie returned before setting it. She rarely set it when home alone. What Heath didn't know wouldn't hurt him. If trouble came, Sharon would deal with it then.

"How is he?" Her gaze searched Karlie's face.

"He'll be fine. Might be home tomorrow." She patted Shadow's head. "Did you enjoy your steak?"

She wagged her tail and licked Karlie's hand. "You are a true treasure, my girl." She glanced at

Sharon. "She's more than served her purpose since joining our family. I can't imagine how we would have been able to do any of this without her." She grabbed the dog's vest from the porch railing, waved at Baines, and entered the house. "Come in so I can set the alarm."

Sharon took her cup inside and closed the door. "Everything's been quiet here. Other than a couple of squirrels chasing each other across the yard, I've seen nothing."

Karlie parted the kitchen curtains. "Don't get lax. With four more of my father's people taken care of, he'll be on the warpath. Wait. I saw something."

"A deer?" Sharon peered over her shoulder.

The alarm blared.

The windows and doors locked.

A blood-curdling scream came from the direction of the trees.

Chapter Fifteen

Karlie grabbed a handgun from a kitchen drawer and checked the ammo. Six rounds. It would be enough. If luck were with them, there was only one man outside, and he would be gravely wounded.

"What are you doing?" Her mother gripped her arm. "You aren't going out there."

"Bad guy or not, we can't let him lie in the pit and bleed to death. Besides, we need someone to interrogate." The man's screams continued. There was absolutely no way they could leave him out there to die that way. It was inhumane.

Her mother huffed. "Fine." She opened the pantry and removed a rifle. "I'll cover you. There's a rope coiled under the back deck."

Karlie froze for a moment. The house had been turned into a fortress with guns hidden in every room. Her mother had lived in fear for twenty years, knowing this day would come. As a child, Karlie had lived free and innocent, unaware of the dangers everywhere, oblivious to the guns. Where had they been hidden then? She shook her head at her naivete.

"We'll have to turn off the alarm." She set the gun down and put Shadow's vest on her, grabbing her own from a peg near the door before taking up her weapon again.

"I'll reset if from my phone once we get outside. We don't want anyone sneaking into the house.

"We'll trigger it and will have to listen to the blaring," her mom said.

"Then we hear it." After the alarm was turned off, she opened the door and slowly stepped outside. When no shots came, she sprinted toward the screams.

A man lay in the pit, a spike through one leg and through his ribcage. A cell phone with a shattered screen lay next to him. Getting him out wouldn't be an easy task.

"Are you alone?" Karlie asked over the noise of the alarm. "Answer truthfully or I'll leave you there to rot and cover you with dirt."

"Now you sound like me." Her mother stepped to her side, the rope over one shoulder.

"Yes. I'm a scout. Please." He lifted a hand toward them. "I need a hospital."

Good luck with that." Karlie stepped back as her mother tied one end of the rope to a tree, then dropped the other end into the pit.

"You'll have to get yourself off the spikes. Hang the loop around your neck, I mean waist." she grinned. "We'll pull you up. It's not going to feel good."

He screamed and slowly pulled himself off the spikes, leaving Karlie to wonder why he hadn't already pulled himself out. Once he was free, his arms fell limp to his sides.

She shouldn't feel sorry for the man, but she did. "Hold on and grit your teeth."

She grasped the rope and, with her mother's help, raised him inch-by-agonizing-inch out of the pit. Propping one shoulder under his arm, her mother taking the other, they dragged him as he slipped in and out of consciousness past a snarling Shadow and into the house.

Once he was in a kitchen chair, Sharon patted him down, finding a knife, a wallet, and a Glock. She set them on the table and went to fetch the first aid kit while Karlie looked for something to use as bandages. They'd make sure he received medical help, but first they needed some answers. She really hoped he didn't die on them. Her conscience couldn't live with that.

"Bite on this." Mom handed him a wooden spoon, then opened the first aid kit. "I've had a little medical training through the years, but I don't have anything to knock you out when I stitch you up. It will hurt a lot."

The man put the spoon between his teeth, his eyes wide. "I need the hospital."

"You'd die before you got there with as much blood as you've lost. If you want more than I can give you, you'll answer my daughter's questions and fast." Mom pulled up a chair and cut away the man's clothes, leaving him in a pair of green boxers stained with blood.

He moaned as Mom poured disinfectant into his wounds. "Put pressure on his leg, Karlie, while I stitch up his side."

The man would die. Karlie couldn't see any way out of him succumbing to his wounds despite her mother's ministrations. She pressed a folded towel to his leg and bit her lip. This was more than she'd ever bargained for. A man's life lay in their hands. They needed Heath's help.

The stranger passed out as Mom probed her fingers in his side looking for a bleeding vein to clamp. "Found it." When she'd stopped the bleeding, she stitched up his side and moved to his leg. "You'd better start with the questions as soon as he's conscious. There may not be much time."

Karlie nodded. "Should we move him to the table? Let him lie down?"

"Don't be too charitable. He would have abducted you in an instant. Still might if he'd been able to relay a message before falling into that pit."

Good point. Karlie patted his cheek rough enough to wake him up. "Where is Anthony Bartelloni?"

"His penthouse in New York, but I'm sure you know that." The man's eyelids fluttered. "He's going to kill me."

"He might, but then we might first," Mom said. "Is it the same place he's always lived?"

"No reason for him to move. The place is a fortress."

"How many more of you are there in Misty Hollow?" Karlie patted his face again. "Stay awake."

"Three."

"Where are they holing up?"

He fastened narrowed eyes at her. "You Bartelloni's daughter or a cop?"

"Answer the question."

"Cheap motel outside of town. They move around a lot to make it harder to be found."

"Good boy." She smacked him again and grabbed her phone to let Baines and Wood know where they'd find Bartelloni's men and tell them to send an ambulance for their prisoner.

When her mother left the room to take care of the bloody rags, Karlie leaned close to him and whispered, "How can I get to my father?"

~

"What do you mean the Marshall women have a prisoner?" Heath raised the head of his bed.

"That's what the text says. Said they've stitched him up, but he needs an ambulance. Also gave the alleged location of his cohorts." Wood grinned. "Want out of that bed?"

"In the worse way." What was Karlie thinking?

While Wood went to find the doctor, Heath winced and sat up. He had a few questions of his own to ask before the man was taken away. Staying in the hospital wasn't an option. He was going to wring Karlie's pretty little neck.

Since Wood was told the doctor wouldn't be around for another hour, Heath dressed and released himself. He didn't have time to wait for formalities. With the help of a crutch, he hobbled from the hospital and into Wood's squad car. He'd call for an ambulance for the injured man once they reached the cabin and he saw the situation for himself.

He turned off the alarm via his phone as they turned into the drive. Before they were out of the car, Karlie stood on the front porch, arms crossed, looking ready for a confrontation. Blood covered the left side of her. Heath hoped it wasn't hers.

"I'll leave you to battle on your own," Wood said.

"I'll get together a force to check out the motel. Good luck."

"Thanks. I'll need it." Heath exited the car and made his way slowly to the porch. "What in the world, Karlie? Can't you stay out of trouble for one day? Tell me that isn't your blood."

"Look who's talking, and no, it isn't mine." She opened the door for him. "I'm surprised to see you home today."

"I wasn't supposed to be home until tomorrow." He narrowed his eyes. "Circumstances changed. Where is he?"

"In the kitchen."

The floor looked like there'd been a massacre, despite Sharon's efforts to clean up the blood. "Is the man alive?"

"Barely," she said, not glancing up. "Ambulance on its way?"

Heath dialed 911 and placed the call. "It is now. Who is he?"

"Wallet's on the table."

He opened the wallet. Daniel Stanetti.

"He fell into the pit," Karlie said from the doorway. "We couldn't leave him there."

"You should have called Wood or Baines. The both of you could have been captured or killed."

"He's alone."

Arguing with her was like arguing with a rock. He'd never met anyone as stubborn as these two.

"Open your eyes, Mr. Stanetti."

The man's lids fluttered. "Can I go to the hospital now? I'd rather take my chances there than with these two. I've never met women so cruel."

"They pulled you out of the pit, didn't they?" Heath didn't blame him, though. "Ambulance is on its way. Mind telling me what your boss is up to?"

"He only wants the two women."

Heath glanced at Sharon. "What does he want with the mother?"

The man shrugged. "Said they both belong to him."

And Bartelloni wouldn't stop until he retrieved what he considered his. "What's the next step?"

"He'll keep on until he has them. He'll send more and more people until the job's accomplished."

Sirens wailed outside.

"Thank God," the man muttered.

Two paramedics rushed into the house. One of them looked at the bandaged man, then to Heath, then to the women. "Someone's first aid most likely saved this man's life."

"I did the work, but it's my daughter who really saved him. I would have left him to die."

"What happened?" The paramedic looked shocked at Sharon's response.

"I wouldn't ask that question," Heath said. "The least you know, the better. This man will be arrested. We'll have a guard placed at his room. I'll be by the hospital later to speak with him." He slowly lowered himself into a chair, exhaustion making standing virtually impossible.

"You should have stayed in the hospital," Karlie said, concern replacing the defiance on her face. "We had it under control."

"I'll be fine after a good night's rest." He leaned his elbows on his knees.

"Take my bed," Sharon said. "I'll take the sofa until you're healed."

"I should argue, but I won't. And I appreciate the offer and accept." He struggled to his feet. "We'll talk more in the morning." His gaze clashed with Karlie's, and he saw a secret there. One he'd have to dig for.

She ducked her head and turned away. "Good night."

After washing his face, Heath grabbed the shorts he slept in from the living room and made his way to Sharon's room as she exited with a small overnight bag in her hand. "Clothes for tomorrow," she said. "There's no point in waking you when you need the sleep."

Mind foggy, he nodded and stumbled into the room, closing the door behind him. Changing into the shorts absorbed the last bit of his strength. A few minutes later, he lay across the bed and passed out.

~

Sharon turned off the alarm and slipped into the night. Outside, she listened to the silence, then headed down the road. If Anthony wanted her, he would have her. On her way to New York, she'd try to devise a plan that would convince him to take her and let Karlie go.

She'd promise to stay, do whatever he wanted, be his arm candy. If he refused, then she'd find a way to kill him.

By the time the sun rose in the morning sky, she slept on a bus headed for a final confrontation with one of the world's most evil men. Whether she lived past that point was to be determined.

Heath would protect Karlie to his dying breath. She knew that now. Sharon had to do her part and convince Anthony to let down his guard. Hopefully, she'd figure how by the time she arrived.

Chapter Sixteen

Sharon marched up to the gold-framed doors of the building where Anthony hid on the penthouse level. She doubted he ever left, content to sit back and let others do his dirty work. A uniformed man stopped her at the door.

"My name is Susan Reece." She willed her voice not to tremble. She hadn't said that name in a very long time. "I'm quite certain Mr. Bartelloni will want to see me."

The man's eyes widened at her name. "He's been waiting a long time for your return." His gaze roamed over the jeans and tee-shirt she wore. "Perhaps you'd like to visit the boutique first?" He arched a brow.

"Yes. A shower would be nice, too." She smiled. "I'll charge the expenses to Mr. Bartelloni. Maybe you could announce me when I'm ready?"

He held the door open, ushering her through with a mock bow. "Good luck, Ms. Reece."

Heads turned as she passed the lobby. The building

might look like a fancy hotel, but she knew it was all a façade. Anthony's minions lived on the other floors. If someone wandered in off the street looking for a room, they'd be told the hotel was full. These men knew exactly who she was.

She squared her shoulders and entered the boutique, heading for a rack of dresses. Anthony had always insisted her clothes be custom made. His lip would curl if she arrived in something off the rack, but it was better than standing in front of him in faded jeans.

Choosing a sheath dress in blue and another in mint green, she ignored the salesgirl and slipped into a dressing room. After trying them on, she went with the green which showed her hair and tanned arms to their best advantage. After purchasing the dress, she headed to the spa.

An hour later, two armed men escorted her to the penthouse. Anthony, still handsome in his mid-fifties, answered the door in a black and silver silk smoking jacket. "Hello, Susan. Where is Kayla?"

"She goes by Karlie now and barely remembers her life before. May I come in?"

He stepped aside, his face expressionless.

The place hadn't changed. Black leather, glass, and gold trim. It looked as it had when she left. No doubt her bedroom had also remained the same. She turned and met his hard gaze. "I'm here to strike a bargain." She folded her trembling hands in front of her.

He struck without warning, backhanding her across the face. "You dare come here without her?"

Putting a hand to her stinging cheek, she nodded. "This isn't the life for a woman raised in a small town.

She's flourishing now. If you love her, you'll let her be."

"She's my daughter." He whirled and headed for a gleaming buffet table where he poured a shot of amber liquid into a crystal glass. "This is where she belongs."

"I'm offering myself in her place with the promise never to leave you again." She hiked her chin as fear churned her stomach.

"What makes you think I want you?" His eyes narrowed.

"The man we interrogated yesterday told me I belonged to you."

A flicker of surprise crossed his face. Good. He hadn't been informed yet of the man's capture and hospitalization. "He fell into a pit of spikes. I seriously doubt he'll live."

Anthony seemed amused. "You've learned a lot in Podunk, haven't you? Booby traps?"

Shrugging, she slowly lowered herself to the sofa, expecting him to tell her to remain standing. She couldn't wait for his orders. If she wanted any leverage, she had to show strength. As if her blood didn't run cold, she casually crossed one ankle over the other. "There isn't much else to do."

"Our daughter is my heir. You're too old now to give me another child."

"So, take a mistress. I won't mind." She tilted her head and gave him a coy smile. "I said I'd do whatever you want, even if it is to remain locked in my room for the rest of my life, waiting to do your bidding."

"All to have me forget about my blood." He paced the room, then whirled and poured himself another shot. "There's never been another woman for me other than you, Susan. Why would I take a mistress? Unlike you, I'm loyal. When I give my heart, I don't take it back. Love is a weakness I should never have given into."

Sharon didn't know how to respond to the pain on his face. She couldn't apologize because she wasn't sorry for taking his daughter away from the life he had to offer. "Where do we go from here?"

His features hardened. "You'll be locked in the room you left so ungratefully until I figure out what to do with you. If you're lucky, you'll accompany me to a fundraiser next week. If not, you'll be tossed into the river."

All she could do was hope his love for her constrained his need for revenge.

~

Karlie paused in the doorway of the living room. The sofa didn't look as if it had been slept in. She turned to the kitchen. No coffee sat in the pot. Her heart plummeted. Whirling, she rushed to her mother's room. "She's gone."

A sleepy Heath bolted to a sitting position on the bed. "What?"

"My mother is gone."

"Hand me my crutch." He slung his legs over the bed, slipping the crutch under one arm and hobbled past her in cotton gym shorts and bare feet. The white bandage around his muscled thigh was a stark reminder of his wound. He turned off the alarm and stepped onto the porch. "She didn't take her car."

"Knowing my mother, she would have walked, taking very little but the clothes on her back. I doubt she's armed. Did she give any sign last night of leaving?"

"She left the room with an overnight bag." He fell into a chair. "Said it was so she wouldn't wake me this morning if I slept in. Why would she go? She has to know Anthony won't want her without you."

"I don't know." Karlie didn't try to hold back the tears and plopped down in the empty chair next to Heath. "She changed when this all started. I'm sure she thinks she can make him a deal to save me."

"Bartelloni doesn't make deals." He exhaled heavily and scrubbed both hands down his face. "I'll notify NYPD and see if they can get to her before she enters Bartelloni's building." He reached over and took her hand. "She'll be okay. We'll get her back. Sharon's smart and resourceful. She escaped him once; she can do it again."

Karlie nodded, enjoying the feel of her hand in his. There was no way to know if she could save her mother, but what she did know was that her father would pay for his crimes if he harmed her. To go through with her plan, she'd have to leave the man she loved. Yes, she loved him. She couldn't deny her feelings anymore; nor could she act on them or let him know how she felt. Slipping her hand free, Karlie stood. "I'll go make coffee."

"Good idea. We'll need to formulate a plan."

Three days. She would stay and help Heath heal for that long, then take Shadow to New York and confront the man she didn't remember. "Do you want me to bring it out here?"

"No, we'll sit at the table." He pushed to his feet, his features twisted in pain.

"Did the doctor give you pain medication?"

"I left without talking to the doctor. I'll be fine."

"Call the hospital while I make coffee and breakfast. Baines can bring you the prescription. Don't be a hero." She swiped the tears from her face, then left him to follow her into the house.

Thankfully, he took her advice and called the hospital once he sat at the table. When he hung up, he glanced at her. "Doctor wants to see me."

"We'll go after breakfast." She cracked eggs into a large frying pan. "I hope you don't mind scrambled."

"That's fine." He crossed his arms, studying her as if she were a specimen. "What's going on in that head of yours?"

"Just worried about my mother."

"It's more than that. You've pulled back, put up a wall between us ever since I got shot."

She shook her head, not trusting herself to speak, and stirred the contents of the pan. To save time, she put a plate of bacon in the microwave and smiled. Mom would have thrown a fit. She hated microwaved anything. Said it wasn't natural and probably unhealthy. "So, what's the plan?" She set a plate of eggs and bacon in front of Heath.

"We head to New York. I'll work with the police department there. Once your father knows you've arrived, he'll come out of hiding."

"Good plan." Not a chance. Heath would never leave her side, and one of her father's minions would kill him in an instant. She'd never get close enough to Bartelloni with Heath beside her. But she'd keep Shadow close, letting her father believe she was a service dog used for anxiety over all that had happened. Karlie could complain that her mother should never have taken her away. Throw her father off guard and take him down. That was her plan. Sounded simple, but she knew it would be anything but.

After breakfast, she insisted on driving to town. The ruse of wearing a police uniform was no longer needed. Instead, she dressed in her customary shorts and tank top and drove her car to the hospital, leaving Shadow tied to a post outside where she could guard the vehicle.

A nurse led them to an office where a disgruntled doctor reprimanded Heath for leaving the hospital early. After examining the wounds, he prescribed pain medication with a warning to stay off the leg and take things easy.

"Hard to do when I'm the sheriff," Heath said.

"Find a way." The doctor handed him the prescription. "Let me know if you need these refilled, and I want to see you in a week."

"Next stop, the station," Heath said when they were back in the car. "I need to let the others know we'll be leaving in a few days."

Karlie tilted her head. "Shouldn't we wait until after your next doctor's appointment?"

He frowned. "Thought you were worried about your mother."

"I am. She's smart. Mom will find a way to convince my father to keep her alive." Please, God, let it be true. "Right now, I'm worried about you."

"Whatever you're thinking, don't do it. Please." He reached over and squeezed her hand. "I couldn't face this world without you, Karlie. You must know that by now."

She did. That's what made it all that much harder. "I'm not planning anything but to follow your lead."

Now, she could add lying to her list of sins. "Let's compromise, then. We'll book flights to New York on Saturday." She'd be on a bus come Friday. One less day to finalize details wouldn't make that much difference.

Chapter Seventeen

Sharon suspected Anthony drugged her each morning when he brought her his coffee. She wasn't completely out of it, but her limbs felt heavier than normal. She forced a smile as he handed her a mug. "Thank you."

"I've decided to let you live." He turned and marched from the room, the loud click of the lock engaging on the door making her blink.

Knowing there were most likely cameras in the room, she pretended to sip the coffee. She'd pour it down the drain after enough time had passed to make him think she'd drunk his offering. Whatever it took to keep his attention on her and off their daughter.

What was Karlie doing that morning? Sharon prayed that her love for Heath would keep her at his side, helping him heal instead of coming to New York. She didn't want her sacrifice to be for naught by her daughter showing up to face Anthony.

After she "finished" her coffee and disposed of the

evidence, she exercised in the small gym attached to her room. Yes, everything was exactly the same as before, except it was more important than ever that she stay fit. Anthony may have said she could live, but she didn't trust him enough to let her guard down. Having to fight for her life was a definite possibility. She stopped as the bedroom door opened, and her old dressmaker entered. "Hello, Alice."

"Susan." The older woman placed several colors of fabric on the table. "I've been ordered to make you a gown for the fundraiser."

"Which charity is he pretending to sponsor now?" She wiped the perspiration from her face with a hand towel.

The woman shrugged. "I'm not paid to ask questions. Which color?"

Easy choice. "The black. I want an off-the-shoulder that skims over my hips and into a mild flare." The other colors were far too cheerful for the situation she found herself in.

"Let's get you measured."

Sharon stripped to her underwear and stood still, letting the woman do her job. As she did, her gaze drifted to a small dot high on the wall. Bingo. She'd located one of the cameras, and her smile widened. She'd locate the others and find out whether her room had a blind spot.

~

Karlie watched from the porch as Heath tossed a ball for Shadow to fetch. He sat on the steps, his injured leg stretched out in front of him. His tee-shirt pulled across the muscles in his back and shoulders. Heath Westbrook was a very handsome man.

143

He'd removed the bandage from his arm where dark stitches held his skin together. The sight of his wounds never failed to send a pang of regret straight through her.

Glancing back to see her watching, he smiled and winked. Her heart leaped. Leaving him would be the hardest thing she'd ever had to do. Why couldn't life have stayed mundane, and she could have met him under different circumstances? She'd fallen asleep the night dreaming of what-ifs.

A question shone in his eyes, fading a little when she returned his smile. Hopefully, he thought her silence only worry about her mother. Wounded or not, if he suspected what she intended to do, he'd find a way to stop her.

He struggled to his feet when Baines pulled up to the house. The deputy exited the car, patting Shadow's head on his way to the porch. "Howdy, Sheriff. Karlie."

"Hello." Karlie approached the railing. "Any word on my mother?"

Baines shook his head. "We didn't find her, but word from New York is that Bartelloni's woman has returned."

"Which means she's with him." Karlie squared her shoulders.

"We presume so. No evidence that harm has come to her. What do you want us to do now, Sheriff?"

Heath leaned on his crutch. "Keep the lines of communication open between us and New York. Karlie and I are headed there this weekend. Once we arrive, we'll take over things there and leave you free to watch over Misty Hollow."

Baines nodded. "Wish I could do more to help.

Good luck to the both of you." He returned to his car and drove off.

"He could have told us that over the phone." Karlie leaned against the railing.

"Guess he thought it best to give bad news in person." Heath climbed the steps, leaning heavily on his crutch. "Wish this leg was healed. I'm not going to be of much use until it is."

"You were shot. It takes time." As horrible as it was, Karlie needed him to remain immobile in order to carry out her plan. "You need to rest for a while. Come, Shadow." She held the door open for him.

He paused in front of her and cupped her face with his free hand. Without a word, he lowered his head and kissed her.

Tears sprang to her eyes. Why did he have to make it so hard? She returned his kiss with all the emotions swirling through her, knowing it might very well be the last kiss she received from him. He'd want nothing to do with her after her betrayal. "This isn't resting," she whispered against his lips.

"Then let's snuggle on the sofa." He chuckled, pressing his lips once more against hers.

"If you're a good boy and take a nap, maybe I'll reward you with a snuggle when you wake up." She ran her hand down his face, stubble rasping against her palm.

"If that's my prize, I'll take a good long nap." He winked and entered the house.

With a long look around the yard, Karlie followed, setting the alarm. While Heath slept, she packed a small bag with essentials, checked her handgun for ammo, and slipped it and a box of bullets into the bag before hiding the bag under the bed. When Heath woke, she'd be gone, deciding not to wait another day. Though, some of his gazes at her were shadowed with suspicion.

After packing, she sat at her desk and wrote a letter. When she finished, Karlie grabbed her bag, left the letter on her desk, and disarmed the alarm. "Quiet, Shadow." They slipped out the backdoor and raced for the car. *Forgive me, Heath.*

~

"Karlie? I'm ready for my reward." Heath entered her room. His glance fell immediately to the white sheet of paper on her desk next to her cell phone. His heart stopped, knowing what he'd read before picking up the note.

My Dearest Heath,

I'm sorry to leave without a word, but I have to go. Please understand. My mother cannot fight my father alone. She needs my help. I've taken Shadow with me. She'll keep me safe.

Please don't come after me. You're in no shape to enter this battle. Stay in Misty Hollow, heal, and I'll see you again.

Karlie

No words of love. He crumbled the note in his fist and tossed it on the desk. Had she been using him this whole time? Toying with his emotions? How could she not know he'd move heaven and hell for her?

He'd suspected she might do something like this but hadn't wanted to believe she'd actually go through with her ridiculous plan. Fighting against the pain in his leg, he hobbled down the hall to his room and tossed clothes into a suitcase. When he finished, he drove to the airport, calling the station as he went.

He was no longer the sheriff of Misty Hollow. It was time to revert back to FBI agent and bring back two fugitives, taking down a mob boss at the same time.

The betrayal of Karlie's leaving ripped at his heart, leaving a gaping wound. How could he have been so stupid as to think they were a team? He could understand Sharon going. The woman hadn't played by his rules from the beginning, but Karlie? She was different than her mother. Guess the proverbial apple didn't fall far from the tree after all.

Heath landed in New York by late afternoon and hailed a cab, heading straight to the FBI offices. He wanted to hurl his crutch across the crowded street. He was worthless without his legs.

"Welcome back, Special Agent Westbrook." A rookie agent glanced up from his desk, surprise on his face. "We weren't expecting you yet."

"Something changed." He limped to the director's office and lowered himself carefully into a chair without waiting to be asked.

"Westbrook." Dirkson raised his brows. "You look a little worse for the wear. Seen some action?"

"A bit." He proceeded to tell of how Karlie Marshall, aka Kayla Reece, had escaped to New York in search of Bartelloni on her own. "I need a way inside the man's building."

"You'll never get in. They know who you are, so undercover is out of the question. Besides, you're unable to do a job in your condition. I'm placing you on medical leave. We'll take things from here."

"No way. I'm not stepping down until those women are safe."

"There's no reason to believe Bartelloni will have them killed. There's a fundraiser Friday night. We'll make sure some agents are in attendance."

Heath would find a way to be there himself. As long as he was still breathing, he'd see Karlie again and have her face him with the truth. Did she care for him or not, or was it all nothing but lies?

Biting his tongue to keep from arguing, he pushed to his feet. Heath had three days to summon enough strength in his leg to throw away the crutch and be useful at the fundraiser. He'd find a way in. Finagle an invitation of his own somehow. Buy his way in.

"Stay out of it, Agent." Dirkson's command followed him down the hall.

Heath hailed another cab to his Fifth Avenue apartment and booted up his laptop. It took some digging, but he found the information needed to purchase a ticket to the fundraiser. Using the name Bill Larson, he paid the five hundred dollars for the ticket. Then, he called down to the concierge to have someone come up and take his tuxedo to the cleaners.

When he'd done that, he stripped down to his underwear and went to bed. Tomorrow, he'd start the painful act of physical therapy until he could walk without the crutch. He'd worry about permanent damage to his leg once Karlie was safe. He wanted to wring her neck. Sleep took a long time coming, despite his exhaustion. He reached over to the nightstand and popped a pain pill, hoping to dull the throbbing in his leg.

Not only had Karlie broken his heart, she'd upended his plans for the future. He liked Misty Hollow, had wanted to remain as sheriff with Karlie by his side. It wouldn't have been difficult to walk away from the FBI and take a permanent position as sheriff. He'd worry about a real re-election next year. They could have bought some land on the mountain and built a cabin of their own. Now, she'd taken all that with her when she'd left.

He flung an arm across his eyes and willed himself to stop thinking and drift to sleep. When he finally did, he dreamed of all his plans lying at his feet and Karlie laughing as she stood next to her father, having chosen that lifestyle instead of the one Heath wanted to offer.

Just a dream, but it lingered with him until morning. Not even the early sun squeezing through the blinds on his window could dispel the raw emotions.

Chapter Eighteen

Karlie showered in the cheap motel room she'd rented the night before, then dressed in stylish pants and a gauzy shirt. She wasn't sure what the rich wore, but she'd seen the outfit on a mannequin at the airport and thought it better than shorts and a tank top when facing her father for the first time.

How had Heath reacted when he'd found her letter? With anger? Sorrow? Karlie shook her head. She couldn't allow herself to be distracted by thinking about the man she'd left behind. All that could be faced when she accomplished the task she'd set for herself.

Dressed, she put her hair into a classy bun, slipped a handgun under Shadow's Kevlar vest which now sported a small badge stating she was a service dog, then took the dog's leash in hand. "Are you ready to face the devil?"

Shadow glanced up at her with big dark eyes as if asking whether Karlie knew what she was doing. Maybe she didn't know exactly, but it was time to end things. Time to put a lifetime of secrets to rest.

She walked to the corner and hailed a cab, giving the driver the address to her father's building. Her knee jerked up and down until Shadow placed her head on her knee. "I'm so glad you're with me." Karlie patted the dog's head, drawing comfort from her presence.

The cab parked in front of a twenty-story building. Karlie smiled and told him to bill Anthony Bartelloni and include a big tip. "It's the least he can do for his prodigal daughter."

Eyes wide, the driver nodded and rushed to open her door. "The ride is on me, Miss Bartelloni."

"It's Marshall, and no, my father can afford to pay. In fact, wait here. You'll receive your payment in a few minutes." Keeping a tight hold on Shadow's leash, Karlie marched to the uniformed man at the front door and told him who she was. "Please pay the driver." Head high, she entered the building.

Every head in the lobby turned to stare. All conversation ceased. A man in a suit rushed to her side. "It's an unexpected pleasure, Miss." He bowed. "Allow me to escort you to Mr. Bartelloni's penthouse."

She gave a slight nod and hiked her chin, doing her best to look haughty as she thought her father's daughter might act. Already the acting grew old and weighed on her. How long could she keep up the pretense of being someone she wasn't? But, she was Bartelloni's daughter, wasn't she?

The man escorted her to an elevator and pressed the button for the top floor. He cut her curious glances but didn't speak again. When the elevator stopped and the doors opened, Karlie told him she'd announce herself. "Thank you."

"My pleasure." She felt his gaze on her as she approached the double doors stained a dark walnut. Karlie pressed a button on the wall and stared into the camera. "I'm here."

The doors opened and she stared into the face she only remembered seeing on the internet. Her father's lips curled into a smile. "I knew you'd come, Kayla."

"It's Karlie now. Where is my mother?"

"You look just like her. So very beautiful." He stepped back so she could enter. "I'll have her brought to us in a few minutes. Don't worry, she's quite safe. Let's spend some time getting acquainted. It's been a long time." He eyed Shadow. "I'll have someone take the dog."

"Shadow stays with me. She keeps me calm." She tilted her head and smiled. "I've been very stressed since you arrived back in my life."

A flicker of anger flashed across his features, but he kept the smile in place. "Perhaps a bowl of water? Food?"

"That would be nice." Karlie sat on a black leather sofa. Shadow plopped at her feet. "What do you want to know about me?"

"Why the change of heart?" He sat across from her and crossed an ankle over one knee. "Your mother won't be pleased to see you."

"I'm sure she won't, but I'm an adult. I came so you would release her."

He shook his head. "I can't do that. She's agreed to stay. Now, I'll have both my gorgeous ladies on my arm at the fundraiser. The fact that both of you are here will bring in the donations. More than I'd dreamed of making." He pressed a button on the arm of his chair and ordered someone to bring champagne, a bowl of water, and the best dog food. "Oh, and bring Susan," he said, almost as an afterthought.

"How did you enjoy giving up all this to live in some small town in the mountains?" He sneered. "Here, you're royalty, not a peasant."

"I loved my life there. I don't think I can ever be happy here. Will you keep me prisoner as you have my mother?"

His gaze hardened. "I trust we'll be able to come to an agreement. At this moment, all I ask is that you stay through the fundraiser. Will you do that?"

She nodded, matching his sharp gaze with one of her own. "I'll need a wardrobe if I'm to stay."

"Anything you want. You're my daughter. People will fall over themselves to do your bidding."

"And I'll hate that."

He shrugged. "Perhaps you'll grow used to it. That is my wish anyway."

She doubted it. The front door opened and the same man who'd escorted her to the penthouse floor brought in food and water for Shadow on a rolling cart. A champagne bottle chilled in a silver bowl of ice next to two crystal flutes.

Her father popped the cork and poured her a flute. "Let's toast your return." He handed her the glass and poured one for himself. "I told you to bring Susan. We'll need another flute."

The man stepped back. "She's in the bath and said she'd be out when finished."

Karlie smiled. Mom didn't appear to do her father's bidding as instantly as his men did. Good for her. "Shall we wait, Anthony?"

A muscle ticked in his jaw. "Call me Father."

"But, you haven't been more than my biological father for twenty years. I'll stick to Anthony. For now." She raised her drink, then took a sip.

His face darkened. Clearly, he wasn't pleased with her insubordination. "It's not hard to see that my blood runs through your veins."

"Would you rather I be a mouse?" She raised her brows.

"No." He laughed. "I like the lioness sitting in front of me."

Wonderful. Karlie had passed her first test.

When the door opened again, Shadow stood and went to greet Karlie's mother.

~

Sharon froze. She couldn't believe her eyes. What was Karlie doing here? Her shoulders slumped. "You shouldn't have come."

"It's good to see you, too, Mom." Karlie's smile held no humor. "You left without saying goodbye."

"That seems to be a habit of hers," Anthony said. He held out his hand, pulled her close, and placed a kiss on her cheek. "All together again."

She fought back a shudder. His touch always left her feeling as if she needed a shower. Sharon pulled her hand free and sat on the opposite end of the sofa from Karlie. Anthony would think he truly was a king now. Sharon had told him more than a few times that Karlie would never show up in New York. Yet, here she was.

"To think that a simple DNA test told me where the two of you were." Anthony set his champagne on a glass-topped end table. "It was fate."

More like bad luck. One of Anthony's minions

154

brought a glass for Sharon and filled it with champagne.

"Come back in thirty minutes," Anthony said. "My daughter has some shopping to do. I'd like you to escort her to the boutique."

Karlie exhaled heavily but didn't speak. She'd have to get used to being escorted everywhere she went if…and it was a big if…Anthony actually let her leave the building.

"How's Heath?" Sharon asked.

"Healing from his wounds, I hope."

"Who is this Heath?" Anthony glanced from one to the other. "A boyfriend?"

Sharon shook her head. "The sheriff of Misty Hollow."

"Ah, the man who caused me so much trouble. He's the type of man I'd like to have working for me."

"He'd never follow orders blindly."

"Mom's right. The sheriff is a very strong man—in body and character."

"Anyone can be bought."

The delusions of a fool. "Since Karlie is here, I'm sure the sheriff is also." Sharon smiled. "Why don't you ask him yourself?" They needed Heath, wounded or not.

"I asked him not to follow me," Karlie said.

"He probably listened as well as you did." Sharon sipped the champagne, the bubbles tickling her nose. "The man took protecting you very seriously."

Anthony called downstairs and told two men to find the sheriff of Misty Hollow and bring him to the penthouse. "We'll see how much it will take to convince the man to our side. Perhaps he'd like to continue in the role of my daughter's guardian. Since my men couldn't get to her, I definitely want him working for me."

~

Heath stared at the two men standing outside his apartment. "Bartelloni wants to see me?"

"Yes. His daughter has returned, and he wants to talk to you."

Could getting close to the man really be this easy? Heath left his crutch leaning against the wall and followed the two men to a waiting Mercedes. Either Bartelloni wanted to make a deal or Heath wouldn't survive the next hour. He'd take his chances.

Ignoring the pain in his leg, Heath entered the building and then the elevator, flanked on both sides by the men. Why hadn't they frisked him? The gun he carried poked his spine. Was it a test of some kind? Both men wore holsters under their suits. He'd seen them when they'd climbed into the car. If he pulled his gun, he'd be dead before he pressed the trigger. No reason to disarm him.

"Ah." Bartelloni stood as they entered. "Welcome, Sheriff Westbrook, or should I say Agent. Please, have a seat. You look like you're in pain."

Heath glanced at the sofa, then limped to the chair opposite Bartelloni. "What do you want with me?"

"I want you to work for me."

Heath frowned. "Why?"

"You kept my men very busy. They couldn't get within fifty yards of my daughter, and my men are very well trained. I'd like you to remain her guardian." He resumed his seat. "There are people who don't like me very much and might try to harm her to get to me."

Heath glanced at a pale Karlie. "I doubt we'd work

well together."

The man chuckled. "Are you speaking of me and you or you and my daughter?"

"Both."

"Hurt feelings over her swift departure, I see." Bartelloni studied his nails. "If you refuse my offer, your life will be forfeited. I'm sure you are aware of that fact."

"How can you be so sure I'd comply with your orders?"

He laughed. "You don't strike me as a man with a death wish."

Shadow left Karlie and placed a paw on Heath's leg. He smiled and scratched behind her ears. "I've missed you, girl." He spoke to the dog, but his gaze drifted to Karlie. "I'm a man who enforces the law. I can't break it working for a man like you."

"I'm only asking you to watch over my daughter, not kill someone. I served my time for my crimes and haven't broken any laws since being released."

"A woman was killed. Your people tried to kill me." Heath turned his attention back to him. "That's not lawful."

"How can you prove such a thing?" Bartelloni smiled. "There is no evidence against me. The men you've killed and arrested were acting on their own. Plotting against me to get to Kay...Karlie ... to use her to bring down all I've built up."

The man seemed sincere, but Heath wasn't buying into his lies. Still, working for the man, even for a short while, would allow him to discover what Bartelloni was up to. Being on medical leave left Heath free to do whatever, as long as the department didn't find out. Or, he could be upfront and let the department know he working for Bartelloni. They needed a man on the inside.

He stood and offered his hand. "I accept."

Chapter Nineteen

Karlie stared at Heath over a rack of clothes. He stood next to one of Bartelloni's other men, dressed in a similar dark suit, face expressionless, like a bookend next to the shop's door. Oh, why had he come? She knew he'd only agreed to watch over her to get close to her father. If Bartelloni suspected anything devious, even for a second, Heath would be killed.

Heath leaned heavily on the dark wooden cane he used now instead of a crutch. He shouldn't be up on his feet.

"I'm tired of this." Karlie turned to the salesgirl. "Just send everything you have in my size, all colors, to my room. I'll try them on there at my leisure." Head high, she marched past her guards and into the lobby, Shadow at her side. Where could she go without feeling like a prisoner? She started for the front doors only to have Heath take her arm and stop her.

"You aren't allowed out yet."

She pulled free. "I'd like some fresh air."

"Perhaps the garden." He arched a brow. "I've heard it's beautiful."

"Why are you doing this?" She crossed her arms.

"You know why." His voice lowered. "We could have come as a team. If I remember correctly, you owe me a snuggle."

As if that could happen now. "With your injuries you should be lying down. A cane isn't enough support."

"It gives me more mobility than the crutch." He leaned closer, his lips near her ear. His breath tickled the small hairs on her neck and sent a shudder down her spine. "I've had it modified to use as a weapon. You're quite safe with me, safer than if I wasn't here."

"I'm safe from my father, yes." She heaved a sigh, shoving down the emotions his nearness caused. "Lead me to the garden." She laughed as he turned to the other man with them and asked where the garden was.

The man turned, headed to the back of the building, and flung open two glass doors. Past them, a flagstone pathway led to a sparkling pool. On the other end of that, an iron gate led to a manicured garden. Karlie felt as if she stepped into a tropical paradise.

"Wow. Money really can buy you anything."

Heath lowered himself to a stone bench. "It appears so, if you look at things through your father's eyes." He pulled a pill bottle from his jacket pocket and swallowed one dry.

"You're in pain." She sat next to him. Shadow, ever faithful, plopped at her feet.

"Go on without me. There's no need for one of us to be by your side here, especially with Shadow with you. I was told the garden is secure." His lips twitched.

"There's no way for you to escape. If you want privacy, this is the only place you'll find it."

"Thank you." She headed down the path past topiaries of zoo animals, rose bushes in full bloom. A weeping willow tree swayed over a koi pond. She sat on a bench and grabbed a handful of fish food from a bowl, tossing the pieces into the water. This place would be her sanctuary while she was in New York.

It wasn't the lake by the cabin or the mountain rising behind it, but it was better than glass and concrete. She leaned against the back of the bench and glanced at the sky, placing a hand on Shadow's head. Unfortunately, doing so dispelled the idea she was alone in nature as skyscrapers rose on each side of her father's building. Did he ever come out here or would he be afraid of a sniper's bullet through one of the windows that faced the garden? Should Karlie even be concerned?

No. Any danger to her would come from the very man who'd fathered her.

"Go ahead and explore, girl." The dog left her side, nose to the ground, seeming happier than she'd been since their arrival. Karlie could relate. New York would never be home.

After half an hour, she pushed to her feet, hoping Heath had recuperated a bit from following her around the store. She might as well head back to her room and play princess by trying on expensive clothes. A dressmaker would be visiting later to fit her for a formal gown. Living a life of luxury would grow tedious very quickly.

Heath stood when she approached. "You found the pond."

"Yes. Thank you for bringing me here. I'd like to go back up now."

He nodded, his gaze searching her face. Heath started to say something, then turned away.

Flanked by the two men, Karlie entered the elevator. Heath and the other man stepped in front of her, blocking the doors when they opened. What did they expect to happen on the penthouse floor? It wasn't as if an assassin could reach anyone there.

"What is your name?" She asked the man next to Heath.

"Miss?"

She quirked a brow and laughed. "Your name is Miss? Seriously, if you're going to be with me all the time, don't you think I should know your name?"

"It's Bruce."

"Nice to meet you, Bruce."

The doors opened and the men stepped out, then led Karlie to the penthouse. Heath reached around her to open the door. His musky cologne filled her senses. What would he do if she turned her head and kissed him?

~

Heath had almost lost his senses when he'd leaned close to Karlie, breathing in the floral perfume she wore. She fit in with her father's world, leaving Heath more lost than he'd ever felt in his life. What if she chose to stay and take over his business when Bartelloni ended up dead or in prison again? Could he go back to being FBI with the possibility of having to arrest her? No. She would never go into a life of crime.

Since Karlie had a dress fitting and wouldn't be leaving the penthouse for a while, Heath had been allowed to return to the opulent room he stayed in until things were over. He removed his jacket, set his gun on the bedside table, and spread out on the thick down comforter.

The department head at the FBI had ranted when Heath said he'd found a way into Bartelloni's empire. Once he'd finished throwing his tantrum, he'd seen reason and agreed to let Heath stay, saying he couldn't guarantee his safety. No surprise there. Heath had disobeyed orders and gone willingly into the lion's den.

Even a blind man could see that Bartelloni cared for Sharon and Karlie. His love for them was his one weakness. All he needed to do was find a way to exploit that love without one of the women getting hurt.

The phone next to the bed rang. "Westbrook."

"Time for lunch. Please come escort us to the restaurant." Bartelloni hung up.

At least he'd said please. Heath groaned and climbed out of bed. He hadn't had near enough time off his leg. He shrugged back into his suit jacket, replaced his weapon in its holster, and grabbed his cane. Gritting his teeth, he headed to the penthouse where the others waited with Bruce. "Sorry. I'm not as fast as I used to be."

"I'll have my personal physician take a look at your leg," Bartelloni said. "I'm sure he can give you something that will dull the pain but allow you to keep your wits about you."

"He shouldn't be up walking around at all." Karlie narrowed her eyes. "But Heath is one of the most stubborn men I've ever met. He's doing permanent damage to himself, I'm sure."

"I'll be fine." Heath motioned his head toward the

door, shoving aside the happiness at knowing she cared about his wellbeing. If he didn't do his job, Bartelloni would replace him. Kill him. The Marshall women would be alone against the man. He couldn't let that happen.

"The doctor will be waiting for us when we return." Bartelloni made a call.

Downstairs, a hostess led them to a private room with a table big enough to seat twenty people. Heath pulled out a chair for Sharon next to Bartelloni, then one for Karlie, choosing the seat next to her. Bruce sat on the other side.

"Is it necessary to have my guards always this close?" She frowned, picking up a menu.

"Yes." Bartelloni slapped a hand flat on the table. "You may live in a fortress, dear, but there are always cracks. Even my men could be bought if the price is right." His eyes twinkled. "Although I do pay them well enough to help them avoid that particular temptation."

The man was right. Bartelloni wasn't the only crime boss in New York. He just happened to be the only one on Heath's radar at the moment.

"Were you able to find a wardrobe of your choosing?" Bartelloni left his menu on the table.

"I bought enough things to break the bank. I'll have the strawberry chicken salad," she told the waitress. "I probably won't wear half of the things I purchased." She gave her father an evil grin. "Hope you can afford having such an extravagant daughter."

"I can." He chuckled. "You're far more willing to spend my money than your mother is."

"Since you won't allow me to go anywhere, why do I need a lot of clothes?" Sharon ordered the same as

Karlie.

Heath went for a juicy fat burger, enjoying the sparring between Karlie and her father. The man had met his match for sure. Despite the hurt of her leaving Misty Hollow without a word, admiration for her spunk filled him. "Perhaps the women would do well with a drive tomorrow," he suggested. "Your vehicles are bulletproof, aren't they?"

"They are." He pressed his lips together and studied Heath's face. After a few minutes of uncomfortable silence, he nodded. "It will do us all good to get out."

Accompanied by a small army, no doubt. What was Bartelloni afraid of? Still, a drive into the country would give Heath time off his feet.

A doctor waited when they returned upstairs. Bartelloni asked the women to return to their rooms to give the men the privacy needed for Heath to be examined.

Heath dropped his pants and took a seat on a kitchen chair. "The stitches finished dissolving this morning."

The doctor poked and prodded. "It appears to be healing well. A clean shot, hitting no bone?"

"Yes, but I thought I'd be moving around better by now."

"It's too soon." The doctor handed him a salve. "Keep this on the healing wound. It will keep it from drying and pulling. You're strong and healthy. I see no reason for you to be bedridden. Keep using the cane or a crutch, and rest when you can." He glanced at Bartelloni, who nodded. "Use the gym to strengthen the muscle."

Wonderful. Whether the doctor's prognosis was true or not, he said what Bartelloni wanted to hear.

Heath met Bartelloni's hard stare. The man might act friendly enough to his men, but he had standards that would be deadly when not met. Heath couldn't let his guard down for a second. It occurred to him that the man's hiring might have been so he could keep as close an eye on Heath as Heath wanted to keep on him.

Once the doctor left, he turned to Heath. "Stay close to my daughter tomorrow. Since her arrival, there's been word of a possible abduction attempt. One of my rivals will use her to bring me down. We cannot let that happen."

"Do you know who?" Heath pulled up his pants. Elephants set up a stampede in his stomach.

"I suspect Langello." He shrugged. "He's wanted my head ever since I ordered the hit on his son twenty years ago for stealing from me. We were once partners, you see."

The man wanted revenge, and Karlie had unwittingly provided the means.

Chapter Twenty

It had been less than a week since her arrival and Karlie was like a child at Christmas with the prospect of escaping what had become a prison. The moment she stepped out of her room, Heath and Bruce moved to her side. Two other men did the same with her mother. Definitely a prison.

Tension rolled off Heath. She glanced up to see determination, and—was that a flicker of fear on his face? "Did something happen?"

"No, and let's hope it stays that way." He took her arm and marched her to the elevator, leaving Shadow to follow. Once they were in the parking garage, Heath had Shadow sniff the limo. "She's trained," he explained to a questioning Bartelloni. "She sniffs out bombs."

"Very good." He gave a smile of approval. "You are full of surprises, Westbrook."

Heath gave the all-clear and opened the door for Karlie to slide inside before getting in after her. "Let's get out of the city," he told the driver.

"You're making me nervous." Karlie narrowed her eyes. "What are you afraid of?" She turned to her father. "Anthony?"

"It's nothing." Her father's smile didn't reach his eyes.

"I'm not a child."

"Very well. We think someone will try to harm you."

"The very man whose son you killed?" Sharon stiffened. "Finding that out was the reason I left. He was only a teenager, barely more than a child."

"He stole quite a bit of money from me, dear. I couldn't let that go unpunished. The boy knew the consequences."

Karlie couldn't believe what she heard. Her father had killed a young man and now that man's father wanted to reciprocate by killing her. Heath would die protecting her. He'd step in front of a bullet. How had things gotten so far out of hand? His coming after her had been a very bad idea. She stared out the tinted window at the city streets. Where would the danger come from? Were they being followed? Would someone confront them when they left the car or would a sniper's bullet slam into her back? "Where are we going?" She turned to Heath.

"A place upstate. It should be safe to walk around there." He kept his gaze out the back window. He gritted his teeth hard enough to crack them.

His alertness affected Karlie, and she moved closer to his side in a vain attempt to feel safe. Would she ever be safe again? Her mother's worry mirrored her own. She constantly glanced out the side windows and the back. Even Shadow sensed the tension. With a whine, she leaned against Karlie's leg.

They drove an hour out of the city before the limo pulled onto a single-lane road and parked in an empty lot of a public park. The men exited the car. Heath motioned for Shadow to come and scouted out the area before letting the women and Bartelloni leave the limo.

"There's a walking path around a small lake." Heath moved to her side. "You should be able to enjoy the day here."

"It is wonderful to be among the trees again." She smiled up at him. "Thank you."

"I hope it's a taste of home, even if a small one." He started to cup her face, then glanced at her father and dropped his hand.

She sighed. Anthony wouldn't consider Heath good enough for his daughter. Not an FBI agent who pretended loyalty but would most likely return to the agency once his medical leave was up. By then, Karlie wanted to be back in Misty Hollow in her simple, often boring life. The thought she'd craved excitement was now ludicrous to her. A slight breeze blew across her face, dispelling some of the fear that had followed them from the city. Ignoring her father's presence, she slipped her hand in Heath's, laughing at his look of surprise. He looked so much like a teenage boy caught kissing the preacher's daughter. Grin widening, she shot Anthony a defiant look.

He narrowed his eyes, then shrugged. No doubt he had worries more pressing than his daughter holding hands with the man hired to protect her.

Shadow's ears perked, and she turned to face the direction they'd come. Heath dropped Karlie's hand

and stepped in front of her, Bruce moving to his side. The two made an effective shield. The other men repeated the process with her mother and father.

Karlie peered down the path but couldn't see or hear anything out of the ordinary. She wanted to reach for the gun under Shadow's vest but didn't want to tip her hand. Leaving that gun hidden could be the very thing that one day saved her life.

Shadow barked.

A shot rang out, slamming into the ground at Karlie's feet. She jumped back with a yelp.

Heath tackled Karlie to the ground as pandemonium ensued.

~

They'd been followed. How could they have been so careless? Heath had kept an eye on the road behind them. He hadn't seen anything suspicious. Whoever had found them was very good.

Karlie squirmed under him. "You're squashing me. Give me a gun and let me help fight."

"Not a chance, sweetheart." He moved, rolling with her and into the slight protection of a fallen tree, his arms tightening around her. "Not quite the snuggle I had in mind." He grinned.

"This is no time for jokes." She shoved against him. "Give me a gun."

"I don't have another one. Stay down." He peered over the log and whistled for Shadow to join them.

"Awesome." Karlie pulled a handgun from under the dog's vest. "Don't tell anyone."

"Clever girl." Heath kept his gaze on the path. He felt sorry for anyone that underestimated the petite redhead. Full of surprises, this woman. Where were those shooting at them?

There. Heath aimed as a man shot from the protection of a tree down the path. A cry of pain let him know he'd hit his target. Now, to find out how many there were.

Karlie fired. Soon, the area sounded like a full-out war.

After the firing ceased, Heath told Karlie to stay put while he checked out who was left unharmed. He climbed painfully over the log. Crouching at the tree line, he joined Bruce and headed to where their enemies had fired from.

One man lay wounded, two others dead. Bruce fired a shot between the living man's eyes.

"Why'd you do that?" Heath scowled. "I had questions."

"Leave no survivors, Mr. Bartelloni says."

"Go check on the others and get out of my way." Heath rummaged through the man's pockets, finding his wallet. He sent the man's identification to headquarters hoping to find out who he worked for, then did the same with the other dead. He returned to Bartelloni's men to discover they'd lost two. "There's no one left to find out who they work for." He shot a sharp glance at Bruce. "We'd best head back in case more are coming." He picked up his cane from where he'd dropped it.

"I agree." Bartelloni put a hand on Sharon's back. "Thank you for protecting my daughter."

Seeing Karlie join them without a gun in her hand, he refrained from telling the man she'd handled her own. "Let's make it quick, folks. We'll be sitting ducks in the parking lot."

He rushed everyone back to the limo and let Shadow do her thing. A frenzied bark alerted him to the fact they had a bomb planted on the undercarriage. "Anyone here know how to defuse?"

They all shook their heads. Bartelloni cursed. "Get back in the trees. I'll have to call for another car."

Which would take at least an hour. Heath glanced around for a safe place to take cover. There was nothing. He led them to a semi-cleared spot behind a thick stand of trees. "Circle the family and keep your eyes peeled."

His cell phone vibrated. A quick glance at the text answered his question. The men worked for Langello. The expression on Bartelloni's face told Heath the man knew who had ordered the kill. "How did they find us?"

His boss shrugged, glancing at one of the men who sweated profusely.

He brought up his gun and aimed at Karlie. Heath's shot took him down. He stood over the traitor in their midst. Bartelloni was right. Everyone had a price. Even Heath. His price had been Karlie. "When did you turn?"

The man groaned. "I'm dying."

"I don't care. You tried to kill your boss's daughter. How much did they offer you? You had to know you wouldn't have gotten away with your attempt just now. Why try?"

"To fail is a death sentence anyway. If I'd killed her, maybe my sister would be spared."

When Bruce moved up to kill the man, Heath blocked him. "No. His price wasn't money but love. We'll get him medical attention and have him arrested." He dared Bartelloni to argue.

The man gave a shrug, his common gesture when making light of a situation. "Let him live. He'll die in prison anyway. I, too, understand the price of love."

As did Heath. Something he intended to tell Karlie when this was over.

Leaving the man where he lay, they waited for the second car to arrive. When they were headed back to the city, Heath made a call to the bomb squad. It would be a disaster for an unsuspecting hiker to stumble across the vehicle and set off an explosion.

Karlie rested her head on his shoulder and fell asleep. He put an arm around her and pulled her close.

"You, too, understand love." Bartelloni met his stare.

"She's the only reason I'm here and not recuperating at home."

He raised his eyebrows. "Will you be able to leave her when you have to return to the agency or will you stay working for me?"

"Karlie won't stay. She'll head back to Misty Hollow. You know that." Heath planned on following her again. To the ends of the earth if he needed to.

"Leaving us both with broken hearts." His gaze drifted to Sharon who snoozed against the window. "Susan won't leave again. She made me a deal."

"Deals are often broken."

"She'll stay." Bartelloni stared out the window, a look of sadness in his eyes. "Reluctantly, but I'll take what she'll give me."

~

Sharon wasn't sleeping. Rather, she worked out the next step in her plan. Tomorrow night was the fundraiser. The time to end things before Karlie got killed.

Would she stay with Anthony once her daughter and those who wanted to harm her gone? He'd treated her with nothing but kindness, despite keeping her a prisoner in the penthouse. Maybe, if he survived, she'd stay. There were worse things in life than being with a man who loved her even if that man ruled an evil empire. She'd suspected from the moment she arrived that the danger to Karlie might come from someone other than Anthony. She'd see the love in his eyes when Karlie had entered the living room that first time.

She had no doubt in her mind that things would come to a boil at the fundraiser. She also knew Heath would do everything he could to protect the woman he loved, even accompany her to Misty Hollow. But, Karlie couldn't leave until Langello was stopped.

Chapter Twenty-One

Tonight was the night to end things. If she lived, Karlie would return to Misty Hollow tomorrow. She missed the cabin by the lake. Karlie wanted to ask Heath to go with her, but his life was here in New York. She smoothed the royal blue gown over her hips and turned a slow circle, glancing in the full-length mirror. The front rose to her collarbone, but the back plunged to her waist. She felt like a princess. "Stay close, Shadow. This form-fitting dress doesn't leave any room to hide a gun."

"You look beautiful." Her mother, wearing black, stood in the doorway.

"So do you." Karlie smiled. "Ready to take down a couple of crime bosses?"

"More than ready." Her mother laughed. "Be careful and stay close to Heath."

"I plan on it." He wasn't the only one ready to make a sacrifice if it came down to it.

The limo chauffeur opened the doors with a

flourish.

Heath's eyes lit up when his gaze landed on Karlie. "Wow," he mouthed.

"You don't look so bad yourself." In fact, he looked quite delicious in his tuxedo.

The limo drove them to an illuminated venue and stopped at the end of a red carpet. Flashbulbs exploded as they exited the vehicle. Shadow whined and pressed against Karlie's leg.

Karlie wanted to relish in her moment of stardom, but Heath took her arm and rushed her into the building. No time to play at being a princess, it seemed. Crime boss or not, her father was respected in the city. Fear, wealth—maybe a combination of both—had drawn in enough people to fill the large ballroom.

Overhead, a large chandelier sparkled. Crystal shone against crisp, white tablecloths. Uniformed servers waited to do the bidding of the guests.

"This is the life you plan on leaving?" her father said. "This could be yours."

"I know where to find it if I want to play." She slipped her arm in Heath's and sailed across the room to the table at the far end. Seated, she glanced around the room. It would be difficult to tell if anyone made them too much attention as all eyes were on the Bartelloni table. Where would the danger come from? A guest, someone who snuck in, or one of the servers? Some of the evening's glitter dimmed.

She'd look up Langello last night and recognized the man the moment he entered the room. His gaze fell on hers. No welcoming smile graced his face. Instead, anger emanated off him in waves. He turned and sat at a table against the wall.

"Why would Anthony invite his enemy?" She glanced at Heath.

"It's all about money tonight." He put his hand over hers. "The devil himself would be allowed to come if he purchased a ticket."

The devil was already there. She shuddered and reached for a goblet of ice water. No wine or spirits for her. She needed to stay sharp.

An orchestra tuned up on a stage, getting ready for the dancing after the meal was served. Her father had spared no expense.

Karlie picked at her lobster. Tension tied her stomach in knots. Sighing, she set down her fork and watched as Shadow enjoyed a steak of her own. "Come, girl." She pushed back her chair. "Excuse me."

"I'll come with you." Heath stood.

"You can't come into the ladies room." She frowned. "I'll be fine."

"I'll wait outside the door." His look told her it wouldn't do any good to argue.

"Fine." She led the way, shooting him an amused look as she pushed open the door.

Inside, she stood in front of the mirror, touching up her lipstick from a tube she'd pulled from the matching clutch she'd brought. The lack of privacy made her yearn for the simplicity of life in Misty Hollow more than ever.

A stall door opened behind her. Through the mirror's reflection, Karlie's eyes widened as a woman stepped out, a gun in her hand.

Karlie dove for the floor, pulling her gun from under Shadow's vest. "Angriff!"

The dog attacked, latching onto the woman's gun

hand, sending her shot wild.

Karlie fired as Heath burst into the room. Her shot caught the woman in the shoulder.

"Down, Shadow." He slammed the woman against the wall. "How many of you are here?"

She spit in his face. "We're everywhere."

"I doubt that. Tell me or I'll let the dog have another go."

Karlie jumped to her feet as the room outside exploded in gunfire. "You might as well talk. My dog is very obedient. She'd attack Santa Claus if we told her to."

By now, Heath had the tip of his cane to the woman's throat. A small blade protruded from the end. "Talk."

"Two servers, a male guest other than myself."

"Bartelloni or Langello?" He pressed the tip against her skin.

"I work for Langello. My target is his daughter. Her parents are targets for the others."

Heath banged her head into the wall. The woman slid to the floor, unconscious. "Party's over. We've got to go."

"My mother needs our help." Karlie opened the door just enough to peek out. "It looks like a war zone out there."

People ran screaming for the exits. Overturned tables provided cover for those shooting at each other. Two servers and one man in a tux returned fire at Anthony's men. "I don't see Langello."

~

Where was Langello? Heath didn't like the fact the man was gone. He didn't seem the type to flee without making sure the ordered hit had been completed.

"Stay behind me." He moved in front of Karlie and opened the door wide enough for them to exit.

From an overturned table, Bartelloni glanced up, relief evident on his face. He motioned for Bruce to join Heath and Karlie. Sharon, gun in hand, sat next to him, blood running down her cheek. Another stain bloomed from her shoulder.

"Mom!" Karlie made a move toward her.

Sharon waved her back. "I'm fine. Get out of here."

Heath grabbed Karlie's hand and made a limping dash after Bruce through the kitchen and out the backdoor. He hoped the others could keep the remaining three assassins covered while he took Karlie to safety.

Bruce held up a hand for them to stop and peered into the street. "Looks clear." A bullet sent him falling back into the kitchen where he stared up with lifeless eyes.

"What now?" Karlie paled.

"I'm calling for backup. We'll stay in the kitchen until they arrive." He shoved her behind a stainless-steel counter and dropped beside her. Shadow would alert them if anyone came in.

"I thought it would be at my father's hand when I faced death. I didn't know about Langello when I came to New York. So many secrets." Tears streamed down Karlie's face. "Now, my mother lies bleeding, and I can't help her."

Heath put his arm around her and pulled her to his side. "Her wound didn't look fatal. Sharon is strong. Don't give up hope."

Nodding, she leaned her head on his chest, only to bolt up when the swinging kitchen doors banged open. She put a hand on Shadow's head to keep her from barking.

"I know you're in here. It's time I got my revenge. The battle is over, and you lost."

Langello. Heath stiffened.

"Imagine my surprise when I learned my rival's mistress and daughter had returned." Footsteps moved closer.

"Angriff," Heath whispered.

Shadow sprang.

A shot rang out.

A yelp.

"Shadow!" Karlie sprang to her feet. "Please, don't kill my dog." She held up her hands.

Heath crawled to peer around the counter. Hopefully, the man thought Karlie hid here alone with only her dog. Shadow lay still. The Kevlar vest had kept the shot from penetrating. Good. Once she got her breath back, she'd resume the attack. Karlie only had to keep the man's attention on her long enough.

Heath moved into position, ready to spring when Shadow did. Please, God, don't let Karlie be killed in the meantime.

"Your son stole from your partner," Karlie said. "It's horrible he died, but it has nothing to do with me. I didn't know any of this existed until a few weeks ago."

"Ignorance is no excuse." The man raised his gun.

Shadow sprang.

Heath fired.

Langello fell. It was over.

Heath climbed painfully to his feet and hobbled to

take Karlie into his arms. "We're done. You're safe."

Shouts came from outside the kitchen. Two armed agents burst into the kitchen. "You two all right? We've secured things outside. You can come out."

Karlie stepped from Heath's embrace and raced away. He followed to find her next to her mother and father.

Sharon knelt next to Bartelloni. From the blood bubbling from a wound in his chest, the man would be a goner in minutes. Sharon cupped his face. "I never stopped loving you. I just couldn't live the life you had to offer."

He put a hand over hers and held the other out to Karlie. "I'd hoped the love of a good woman could save me. I was a fool. The penthouse is yours, Sharon. My empire has crumbled. The two of you will never want for anything again."

Karlie took his hand. "I'm so glad to have met you before—"

His eyes drifted closed. "Me, too."

"No." Sharon put her fingers to his throat, checking for a pulse, then burst into sobs.

Turning, Karlie buried her face in Heath's chest. Her arms wrapped around his waist.

He leaned his chin on top of her head. "Let's get you home, and your mother medical attention."

Hours later, they sat next to Sharon's hospital bed where she slept. "What will you do now?" Karlie asked.

"I suppose you'll be headed back to Misty Hollow."

"Yes." She raised a red-rimmed gaze to his. "I suppose you'll stay."

"I have work to do here." He reached for her hand

181

only to have her pull away.

"Mom wants to stay here and start a new business. She said Bartelloni Tower should be a proper hotel. I don't want the city life." She stared at her mother's face. "I'll miss her."

Would she miss him? "She'll do well." He cleared the lump forming in his throat.

"What will happen to those who worked for my father?"

"They're being rounded up. Regardless of your father's saying the contrary, these men have killed. They belong behind bars."

"You'll be able to finish healing." She folded her hands in her lap. "The cabin is the best place for me to forget what has happened. The secrets are exposed now. I'm ready for my simple life back."

So, it was goodbye. He lowered his head and placed a tender kiss on her cheek. "Be careful." Straightening, he marched from the room, tears of his own running down his face. He'd wanted her to ask him to go with her. He'd wanted to offer. But, he was truthful in saying he had things to take care of here. Outside, he hailed a cab. Despite the late hour, he'd been ordered to headquarters for a briefing.

"Will you actually take your medical leave now?" The department head quirked a brow.

"Yes." Heath smiled sadly. "I'll have my leg looked at and follow doctor's orders this time." Heath had fulfilled his task of keeping Karlie safe. He had more to heal than his leg. His heart lay in shattered shards, heavy in his chest. He rubbed his hands roughly down his face and headed to the apartment that no longer felt like home.

Epilogue

Six months later

Karlie sat on the front porch of the cabin and gazed through the rain at the lake. One hand rested on Shadow's head, the other held a cup of hot coffee against the chilly spring morning. Life had settled into a pleasant routine, if a bit lonely. She didn't have to work, not with her inheritance, but she'd resumed her job as waitress at the newly-built diner. Weekly conversations with her mother showed everything was good in New York.

Karlie even saw Heath on occasion when he came into the restaurant. It helped Karlie to know he no longer limped, and no permanent damage had been done to his leg. Oh, how she missed him. She huffed and pushed to her feet. As she turned to go, she spotted someone coming up the road, shoulders hunched against the rain.

Shadow dove off the porch and took off at a sprint. Heath? Karlie dropped her mug, spilling the coffee and shattering her favorite mug.

Stooping to wrap his arms around the dog's neck, his gaze met Karlie's. Her breath hitched. He'd come.

"You're wearing a sheriff's uniform," she said, as Heath approached. After six months, that's the best she could come up with?

His lips curled into a smile. "Meet the new permanent sheriff of Misty Hollow."

"Where's your car?"

"Flat tire about a mile from here." He stopped at the bottom step. "May I come up? It's raining pretty hard."

She nodded. "You're staying?"

"If you'll have me."

She jumped off the porch and into his arms. "I thought you'd never get here."

He held her tight. "I love you, Karlie. There's no way I could stay away." He carried her out of the rain.

"But, you said you had to stay in New York."

"No, I said I had work to do. That meant an apartment to sell, a job to quit, another to find. My leg took longer to heal than I'd thought. I didn't want to limp to you, I wanted to run." He cupped her face. "Do you still want me?"

"More than anything. I love you, Heath Westbrook. From the whining coming from my dog, she does too." She laughed. "Why haven't you kissed me yet?"

"You still owe me a snuggle on the sofa, if memory serves me correct. My reward is far overdue."

"Then come on in."

Heath carried her inside and set her down, lowering himself to the space next to her. "I plan on snuggling with you for the rest of my life."

She caressed his face. "I like that idea." She raised

her face to his and lost herself in his kisses.
The End

Enjoy the first chapter of Deceptive Peace.

Chapter One

Her mother had once told her that Misty Hollow was the perfect place for someone to go who didn't want to be found. Sierra Wells wanted to disappear off the face of the earth.

When her mother had dropped the bombshell that the man Sierra almost got engaged to was actually her half-brother, a baby she'd given up for adoption, well...What a secret her mother had kept the eleventh hour. What if she'd died before letting Sierra know?

She pounded the steering wheel. Dear brother Dayton accepted the fact less graciously than Sierra had and said it made no difference to him. Sierra was his.

How dare he? She belonged to no one but herself. Only now, he'd grown violent, and she'd fled to the middle of absolutely nowhere, a town deep in the Ozark mountains. Talk about insane.

The car's headlights barely cut through the inky darkness. A mountain road that time of night might not have been a good idea, but Sierra hadn't wanted to stay another day where her brother could get her in his claws. No, Misty Hollow sounded perfect to her, and she'd found the cutest little house online. She even had a job waiting for her at the local coffee shop.

Heavy clouds overhead released their burden making visibility less. Sierra slowed her speed and leaned forward as if she could peer through the spaces in the raindrops. She glanced at her GPS. Nothing between her and her new home but dirt roads branching off the one she drove on. She had no choice but to keep driving.

Something slammed into her front bumper sending her car spinning. Sierra screamed and stomped on the brake as the car skidded into a ditch. Her head snapped forward, colliding with the steering wheel.

She sat there, fighting to catch her breath. What had she hit? Please, God, don't let it be a person. Don't be stupid. Why would a person be out on a night like this? She had to go check.

She shoved her car door open and stepped into the downpour. She sloshed her way out of the ditch, slipping several times in the process, until she once again stood on firm ground. A doe, its neck at an odd angle, lay on the embankment. Sierra turned and searched the trees behind her.

Her heart dropped as a spotted fawn stepped from the trees. "I'm so sorry, little one." Her words broke on a sob. "We're both in a pickle now."

There was no way she'd get her car out of the ditch short of a tow truck. She slid down the hill to the ditch and fished her cell phone out of her purse. No reception. Should she start walking or hope another vehicle would come by? Could she trust anyone that stopped? She'd seen too many times on the news how a woman out alone vanished without a trace. She sat in the driver's seat out of the rain and turned off both the lights and the engine. Her car would be the trace, should she disappear. Unless a serial killer tow-truck driver came around.

She glanced up and screamed. A man stood near the dead doe.

He laid his rifle on the ground and held up his hands. "Are you okay?" His words barely pierced the pouring rain.

"There's a fawn!" She pointed. She was definitely not okay. She put a hand to her head, bringing her fingers back sticky. When she looked up again, the hooded man stood next to the car.

"You're bleeding." His voice was softer than she'd thought.

"Thank you, Captain Obvious. I'm sorry. I'm a bit shook up. I don't mean to be rude."

"Apology accepted. Come with me."

"Uh, you're a stranger."

"If I was going to harm you, I'd have done so already. I'm not going to let the doe go to waste. You'll have to lure the fawn. I live a mile into the woods."

She grabbed her purse and the overnight bag she'd tossed in the backseat and returned to the rain filled nightmare of a night. "Come on, darling. Follow your mama."

The man hefted the doe onto his shoulders with a grunt. "Grab my gun."

Okay. Maybe he really did mean her no harm. She picked up his weapon and obediently followed. "Will my car be alright out here?"

"Who is going to steal a wrecked vehicle?"

Point taken. She couldn't get over how fast he moved with a deer on his shoulders. She'd never manage to drag it more than a few feet.

How much farther? Her feet sank into puddles with every step. Her bag grew heavier as the clothes inside got wet.

Finally, she could make out a light through the rain

and followed the stranger into a small clearing. He marched to a cement slab, cut holes in the doe's legs, and reeled her up on some contraption.

"Go on in, take a shower, make yourself comfortable. I'll be skinning the deer for about half an hour."

"What about the fawn?"

"I'll have to take care of her until she's big enough to fend for herself."

"What's your name? I'm Sierra Wells."

"Spencer Thorne."

Dismissed, she entered the cabin. Masculine with plaid throws on leather furniture, a crude wooden table that looked handmade, a small but functional kitchen. Two doors stood closed on the opposite wall. The first one led to a bedroom with a rugged four-poster bed. The second was the bathroom. The whole cabin was as big as her mother's living room.

Sierra dug in her overnight bag for the least wet of her things and turned on the shower. Before getting undressed, she turned the lock on the door, then leaned against it. What was she doing? She ran from one crazy man straight into the home of a stranger. What if this Spencer was as unhinged as Dayton?

~

While he had been out hunting, Spencer hated to see a fawn orphaned. It wasn't the woman's fault, but he still had to squelch his anger at the sight of the poor animal watching him with big eyes.

Now, the woman was in his house. He didn't like people. Avoided them as much as he could, but he couldn't leave her on the side of the road. Even Misty Hollow had its kooks.

Once he finished skinning and cutting up the deer, he tossed the parts he couldn't eat into a wheelbarrow and carted them to the edge of his property for the wild animals to enjoy. Then, he entered the house to the sound of the shower. Hopefully, she wouldn't use all the hot water. He got his electricity from solar panels, not wanting to be connected to the grid in any way. Except for his cell phone. His one luxury.

He grabbed a can of condensed milk from the cupboard. The fawn wasn't the first orphan he'd had to care for. He poured the milk into a bowl and set it on the corner of the porch. Hopefully, the little thing would eat.

Satisfied he'd done all he could at the moment, he went to his room and changed into a pair of flannel pants and a tee-shirt. His stomach rumbled, reminding him he hadn't eaten in a while. He frowned at the sound of the shower still running. Shaking his head, he grabbed eggs and bacon from the fridge.

When Sierra emerged from the bathroom, he said, "Solar panels provide my power. Long, hot showers are a luxury I don't have."

Her eyes widened. "I'm sorry. I didn't know. Can I trouble you for a ride home?"

"Sorry. Truck needs a new battery. I have the battery, but I've been out in the deluge long enough tonight. You're welcome to eggs, bacon, and the couch."

"Do you have a drier?" She clutched her wet bag.

He shook his head, cracking eggs into a bowl. "Line dry."

She sighed and set the bag next to the couch. "I've rented a place in Misty Hollow. Fully furnished, thank goodness." She sat in one of the kitchen chairs. "I start a job at Still Brewin' on Monday."

Spencer wasn't good at small talk. Instead, he preferred silence, which is why he lived alone except for Buster. "Can you let my dog in? He wandered off while I was hunting."

"Absolutely." She jumped up and opened the front door.

Buster, a large mixed breed dog, entered and shook, spraying Sierra.

The outrage on her face made Spencer smile. He ducked his head to hide his amusement. "He's harmless unless you try to hurt me."

"What if you try to harm me?" She returned to her seat.

"He'd help." He ducked his head to hide the twitching of his lips, then glanced up again.

Her face paled, and she stared at her hands folded on the table in front of her. After a few minutes, she wondered the cabin looking at and touching his things. Pretty woman. Hair the color of honey that fell past her shoulders. Hazel eyes that reflected her emotions by changing from green to blue and every shade in-between. Petite and slender, but curvy in all the right places. The men in town would be swarming like ants to a piece of white bread.

"Here." He set a plate of bacon and scrambled eggs on the table, then fixed a plate for himself.

"Why don't you have any pictures?" She sat across from him.

"No need."

"You look military. Are you?"

"Was."

She sighed and started eating. He didn't like to be rude, but conversation seemed a waste of time when he doubted he'd see her again unless they passed on the street. No sense in exchanging information. He liked his peace and solitude and wanted nothing to change.

"I'm moving to Misty Hollow to make a fresh start. Are the people friendly? What about the local police? Are they capable?"

He jerked his gaze toward her. "That's an odd question to ask. Are you bringing trouble to our town?"

"No." She lied. He could tell by the look in her eyes. "But I am a woman living alone."

"The sheriff used to be FBI. He's quite capable." He narrowed his eyes. For the first time in a long time he wanted to know more about a person. What really brought this woman to Misty Hollow?

He tossed a piece of bacon to Buster. "We've had our share of trouble, but Misty Hollow is a nice place to live."

"I like how secluded it is." She forked eggs into her mouth.

Another strange statement. The woman seemed to be hiding. From what or from whom? Don't get involved, Spencer. Pretty women were always trouble. Keep your distance. Her problems were not yours.

When they'd finished eating, he gathered the plates and carried them to the sink. "You can use the blanket on the chair. Go ahead and get some sleep. I wake early." He washed the dishes and stared out the window.

The rain had lessened. Good. He should be able to replace the battery in his truck in the morning and get Sierra out of his house.

He stopped at the sofa and stared into her sleeping face, noting tear tracks on her face that had left the hair near her temple damp. His heart lurched. The woman was hurting, and he'd always had a soft spot for hurting creatures.

Dear Reader,

I hope you enjoyed Heath's and Karlie's adventure. If you enjoyed *Secrets of Misty Hollow*, please leave a review. Reviews are priceless to authors.

May your life be full of adventure and love.

Cynthia Hickey

Website at www.cynthiahickey.com

Multi-published and Amazon and ECPA Best-Selling author Cynthia Hickey has sold close to a million copies of her works since 2013. She has taught a Continuing Education class at the 2015 American Christian Fiction Writers conference, several small ACFW chapters and RWA chapters, and small writer retreats. She and her husband run the small press, Winged Publications, which includes some of the CBA's best well-known authors. She lives in Arizona and Arkansas, becoming a snowbird, with her husband and one dog. She has ten grandchildren who keep her busy and tell everyone they know that "Nana is a writer".

Connect with me on FaceBook
Twitter
Bookbub
Sign up for my newsletter and receive a free short story
www.cynthiahickey.com

Follow me on Amazon

Enjoy other books by Cynthia Hickey

Brothers Steele
Sharp as Steele
Carved in Steele
Forged in Steele
Brothers Steele (All three in one)

The Brothers of Copper Pass
Wyatt's Warrant
Dirk's Defense
Stetson's Secret
Houston's Hope
Dallas's Dare

Fantasy
Fate of the Faes
Shayna
Deema
Kasdeya

Time Travel
The Portal

Tiny House Mysteries
No Small Caper

SECRETS OF MISTY HOLLOW

CYNTHIA HICKEY

CLEAN BUT GRITTY Romantic Suspense

Highland Springs

Murder Live
Say Bye to Mommy
To Breathe Again
Highland Springs Murders (all 3 in one)

Colors of Evil Series

Shades of Crimson
Coral Shadows

The Pretty Must Die Series

Ripped in Red, book 1
Pierced in Pink, book 2
Wounded in White, book 3
Worthy, The Complete Story

Lisa Paxton Mystery Series

Eenie Meenie Miny Mo
Jack Be Nimble
Hickory Dickory Dock

A Heart of Valor
The Game

SECRETS OF MISTY HOLLOW

Suspicious Minds
After the Storm
Local Betrayal

Overcoming Evil series
Mistaken Assassin
Captured Innocence
Mountain of Fear
Exposure at Sea
A Secret to Die for
Collision Course
Romantic Suspense of 5 books in 1

INSPIRATIONAL

Nosy Neighbor Series
Anything For A Mystery, Book 1
A Killer Plot, Book 2
Skin Care Can Be Murder, Book 3
Death By Baking, Book 4
Jogging Is Bad For Your Health, Book 5
Poison Bubbles, Book 6
A Good Party Can Kill You, Book 7 (Final)
Nosy Neighbor collection

Christmas with Stormi Nelson

The Summer Meadows Series

CYNTHIA HICKEY

Fudge-Laced Felonies, **Book 1**
Candy-Coated Secrets, **Book 2**
Chocolate-Covered Crime, **Book 3**
Maui Macadamia Madness, **Book 4**
All four novels in one collection

The River Valley Mystery Series
Deadly Neighbors, **Book 1**
Advance Notice, **Book 2**
The Librarian's Last Chapter, **Book 3**
All three novels in one collection

Historical cozy
Hazel's Quest

Historical Romances
Runaway Sue
Taming the Sheriff
Sweet Apple Blossom
A Doctor's Agreement
A Lady Maid's Honor
A Touch of Sugar
Love Over Par
Heart of the Emerald
A Sketch of Gold
Her Lonely Heart

Finding Love the Harvey Girl Way

SECRETS OF MISTY HOLLOW

Cooking With Love
Guiding With Love
Serving With Love
Warring With Love
All 4 in 1

A Wild Horse Pass Novel
They Call Her Mrs. Sheriff, book 1 (A Western Romance)

Finding Love in Disaster
The Rancher's Dilemma
The Teacher's Rescue
The Soldier's Redemption

Woman of courage Series

A Love For Delicious
Ruth's Redemption
Charity's Gold Rush
Mountain Redemption
Woman of Courage series (all four books)

Short Story Westerns
Desert Rose
Desert Lilly
Desert Belle
Desert Daisy
Flowers of the Desert 4 in 1

Contemporary

Romance in Paradise

Christmas

The Red Hat's Club (Contemporary novellas)

The Red Hat's Club 3 – in 1

Short Story

One Hour (A short story thriller)
Whisper Sweet Nothings (a Valentine short romance)

Made in the USA
Middletown, DE
28 July 2023

35803831R00125